PUSHING HIS
Luck

PUSHING HIS
Luck

KIRA ARCHER

Entangled Publishing, LLC
2614 South Timberline Road
Suite 105, PMB 159
Fort Collins, CO 80525
rights@entangledpublishing.com

Indulgence is an imprint of Entangled Publishing, LLC.

Edited by Alethea Spiridon
Cover design by Bree Archer
Cover photography by EXTREME-PHOTOGRAPHER/Getty
Images

Manufactured in the United States of America

First Edition September 2019

To my husband.

I regret to inform you that our luck is shite and as we still haven't won the lotto, we might need to come up with a new retirement plan.

And to Taco Bell, for building a location half a mile from my house and without whom my children would have starved while I wrote this book.

Chapter One

Charley Claybourne turned into the nearest store and hightailed it to the dairy section. She needed some chocolate milk. STAT.

Well, the lactose-free variety. Her stomach had enough issues dealing with her anxiety over her upcoming meeting without trying to process dairy.

Her phone buzzed, but she ignored it. Someone walked by the cooler and grabbed a quart. There was one left. Only one. And that baby was hers.

She picked up the pace and reached for the last jug on the shelf, her fingers wrapping around the handle just as a larger set of fingers wrapped around the bottom of the jug.

She sucked in a breath and pulled lightly, testing the other person's determination before she looked up to pin the would-be milk thief with a glare. He didn't let go.

"Excuse me, but I believe I had that first."

Her phone buzzed again, and she yanked it out of her pocket, silencing it with a groan. "I believe you're mistaken," she said, trying to keep it civil. After all, the poor man on the other end of her jug couldn't possibly know he was about to ruin her already stressful day. "I clearly had it first."

Her phone buzzed a third time, and Charley shot the tall, vaguely familiar-looking Thor lookalike a mild glare before glancing at her phone to see who was blowing it up. Izzy. Of course. Because Charley was late, an issue not helped by the sweaty beefcake on the other end of her chocolate milk.

"No, I'm pretty sure I had it first," he said, his deep, slightly gravelly voice drawing her attention from her phone.

She looked up at him, freezing for a second. He looked a lot like...naw, his hair was too long, and he was more muscley than—

Her phone buzzed again, and she swore under her breath and answered. "Izzy, I'm on my way. I just had to grab something from the store."

As soon as she dealt with the imminent brawl that was about to break out over the last jug of Choco-Lact-Ish. She wasn't leaving without her crutch of choice.

She nodded her head at her fingers wrapped around the handle. He returned the gesture, nodding at his own hand with a firm grip on most of the rest of the jug.

She interrupted Izzy's constant stream of chatter in her ear. "I gotta go, Iz. I'll be there in fifteen. Just need to pay for my milk."

She hung up and renewed her grip as the guy at the other end of the jug raised an eyebrow.

"I think we're going to have to agree to disagree on the whole *your milk* thing."

She gritted her teeth to keep her jaw from dropping open. Was this guy really going to fight her over a jug of chocolate milk?

"Look, not to go all cliché and stereotypic on you, but isn't chocolate milk a bit too kid-friendly of a drink for..." She looked him over, from the top of his spiked blond hair to his easily size fifteen or more feet. "Someone who's obviously *not* a kid?"

"How do you know I'm not buying it for my kid?"

She frowned. She'd never considered herself to be one to take milk from a baby, but dammit, there were special circumstances today.

"*Are* you buying it for your kid?"

He flashed a brilliantly white grin that had her knees shaking. Or maybe that was the hunger. She hadn't eaten all day.

"Unfortunately, no," he said. "However, chocolate milk happens to be an amazing post-workout beverage. Helps keep my muscles from seizing up and replenishes faster than other drinks, according to my trainer. I didn't really pay attention after the words 'chocolate milk is good.' That sold me. All I know is it tastes amazing and does a body good." He ran a hand down abs that were obviously—even through his well-fitting shirt—toned and rock hard and winked at her. She gave him what probably looked like a spooked owl blink in response.

Was this guy for real? To be fair, he wasn't wrong. It was *so* doing him good. He must be bathing in the stuff. But still. *Focus!*

"So, get the regular chocolate milk. Why do you need the lactose free?" she asked.

He shrugged. "I don't know. Trainer says to get lactose free, so that's the kind I get." He tugged a little, but she didn't let go. "What about you? Do *you* have a houseful of milk-deprived children waiting at home?"

His brilliant blue eyes sparkled down at her, but she wasn't going to give in to their power. Power he was obviously used to wielding. Damn, the Disney Prince smolder was strong with this one. Only the thought of something cool, thick, and chocolatey filling her anxiety-ridden and sadly empty tummy could fight those baby blues.

She renewed her grip on the jug. She really didn't want to get into this with a stranger, especially not an insanely good-looking one she'd normally be trying to impress, but time was short and so was her patience.

"No. I'm buying it for myself because I haven't eaten all day, I'm stressed out of my ever-lovin' mind, and I've only got about two minutes to cram some sustenance into my face before I have to jet to a really important business meeting."

"And chocolate milk is the answer to all your ills?" he asked, that disconcerting smile still in place, which was making it really hard to stay mad at him.

"Yes, it will. It'll fill my stomach, the chocolate will calm my nerves, and I need the lactose-free brand because—"

She stopped short, horrified she had nearly told him all about the ill effects dairy tended to have on her system. Especially when she was anxious.

His smile broadened, obviously grasping her gassy meaning. She gripped the jug so hard her knuckles turned white, wishing on whatever gods happened to be listening that the floor would open up and swallow her. Or, better yet, swallow him. Then she could get her milk and get the hell out of there.

Her phone dinged with a reminder that her meeting started in an hour.

Ugh. Forget it. He could have the damn milk. She'd chug some water and pretend. She didn't have time for this.

But before she could push the jug toward him, he let go. And since she still had a tighter-than-average grip on it, the sudden absence of resistance sent the jug flying. It crashed to the floor behind her, the plastic making that unmistakable cracking sound followed by the ice-cold whoosh of her chocolate salvation splashing up the back of her clothes and leaking all over the floor.

"Oh wow, I'm so sorry," he said with a chuckle. "I thought you had a good grip on it."

Charley closed her eyes and took a deep breath. There was no way her life was this cursed. She'd always had bad luck. She'd pull the one box off the shelf that was missing parts, her luggage always got lost or damaged when she flew, and her tires would find any nail in a ten-mile radius of her car. She once moved her car in a windstorm so the trees she'd been parked under wouldn't fall on her car only to have her neighbor's tree fall into her driveway and crush it anyway.

She was used to the ridiculous things that happened to her and let the running inside joke that was her life slide off her back most days.

But the fact that she was standing in the dairy section on the verge of crying over literal spilled milk on the most important day of her professional life had to be some violation of the universe's cruel and unusual punishment laws. The fact that she was doing so in front of the most drop-dead gorgeous man she'd ever been within eyeshot of was just the icing on top of the world's most craptastic cake.

"I really do apologize," he said, though it would've sounded much more sincere if he hadn't been trying to hold back his laughter until he was red in the face. "I was trying to let you have it."

Yeah, he'd let her have it all right. Lovely. "It's all right. Totally my fault."

An irritated employee had already put up a caution cone and slapped a mop into the mess, splattering more dirty milk all over her. She didn't even complain. She'd have been pissed to have to clean up that mess, too. She apologized profusely, her cheeks flushing with embarrassment and frustration. She was still freakin' hungry and stressed and… Her phone dinged with another reminder she needed to get her ass moving.

Crap on a cracker. She needed to go. Maybe Izzy would have something in her fridge that wouldn't kill her stomach. And something in her closet she could change into because milk splattered clothes were *not* going to make a great impression.

Her milk thief, meanwhile, looked like he was going to try and keep the conversation going. She gave him a weak smile and backed away.

"If you'll excuse me," she muttered. She gave him a weird half nod and hightailed it out of there.

If a simple trip to the store for some milk ended in this kind of spectacular disaster, it definitely didn't bode well for the rest of the day.

Her cousin Izzy's new penthouse wasn't too far away. Closer than her own small apartment. She could go there and get cleaned up and still make it to the Lachlan building before her conference with Christopher Lachlan and his board.

She couldn't screw up this meeting. If she didn't get this account, her fledgling business would never get off the ground.

Her stomach growled and twisted, and she picked up the pace. That chocolate milk would have gone a long way to make her whole day a lot better. Stupid to hang so much on one chocolatized beverage, but it was what it was. Some people smoked, some drank. She did chocolate milk.

She made it to her cousin's in record time and pounded on the door. Izzy took one look at her and stepped to the side while Charley made a beeline for the kitchen. She spilled the whole story while raiding the fridge—no chocolate milk but there was grape juice, which would have to do—and plucking at her milk-splattered clothes to hold them away from her now clammy skin. Izzy was, understandably, beside herself with laughter.

"Thanks for the support there, Iz," Charley said.

"I'm sorry, but seriously…" Her words cut off as she barked out another laugh. "I mean, only *you* could go to the store for something simple and somehow get in a drag-out fight with some male supermodel over fake chocolate milk and end up covered in it."

Charley ignored her and started sucking juice right from the pitcher.

The sound of a picture being taken made her look up even though she kept on drinking. Until she saw her brother, who was now chuckling over the picture on his phone.

"Derrick!" Charley shouted.

"Sorry, sis. Couldn't pass up that opportunity. You look like you've been rolling around in a cow pen."

"You little…get back here!"

"Sorry, can't hear you!" he said, laughing and hurrying from the room before she could chase him.

She glared at the door but didn't go after him. That *can't hear you* bit always sent a bolt of shame and guilt through her. He meant it as a joke, but she had a hard time taking it that way. It was her fault they'd gotten into that accident in high school. Her fault he'd lost an ear in the process and had problems with retaining information sometimes. He didn't blame her, but it didn't matter. She blamed herself and always would. So, she let him get away with murder.

"All right, I've got to get out of these clothes," she said, pulling at her clothes as she put the pitcher back. "I'm soaked."

She headed down the hall to Izzy's room and yanked off her top, swearing when she noticed that the milk had soaked through to her bra.

Izzy crinkled her nose. "Good riddance," she said, nodding to the sports bra Charley wore. "That thing is hideous."

"It's also supportive and comfortable."

"And now it's ruined, so take it off and you can put this on," she said, holding up a padded bra that looked like a really expensive, silky soft torture device. But Charley didn't have time to argue.

She gripped the bottom of her bra and started shimmying it up over her head. Easier said than done. Sports bras were not known for their ease of removal. Add some moisture and…it really didn't go as well as Charley hoped.

"Damn, I think I'm stuck," Charley said, twisting her body as if that would somehow remove the tight elastic from its death-hold on her face.

Izzy was nearly peeing herself at this point, and Charley glared at her with the one eye that could peek through the armhole of the bra. "I could use some help!"

"Breathe, Chuck, breathe!" Izzy said when Charley groaned through the material.

She finally ripped the thing off her head and tossed it. "Thanks. I could've smothered."

Izzy laughed again. "Hey, I'm always there for you, Chuck, you know that. You got a body you need buried, just call. But I draw the line at bra removal."

Charley rolled her eyes and put on the clean bra that Izzy threw to her. "Got an outfit I can borrow?"

Izzy grinned through another laugh. "Sure. Though I think Cass's stuff would be more your taste. Let's raid her closet."

Izzy led Charley back to her roommate's closet and threw the double doors open wide. "Take your pick."

Charley blew out an appreciative breath at the bounty before her and stepped inside.

"What was Derrick doing here?" she asked, gently touching the sleeve of one dress before moving on to another.

"I had some tickets for that hockey game he wanted to go to, so he was picking them up."

"Good. Because if he posts that picture, I need to know where I can find him."

"Ha! Right. You've been trying to keep that boy under control his whole life. Give it up."

"Yeah, yeah." Like she needed to be reminded there was one more thing she couldn't control.

Charley wandered back and forth in Cass's massive closet, slowly going through the gorgeous clothes.

"Quite the selection," she said, glancing over her shoulder at her cousin, who shrugged.

"The first few months after we got the money, we had a little more fun than we should've at the boutiques."

The money in question being the lotto Izzy won with Cass and their friend Kiersten. Charley would be lying if she said she wasn't jealous, though she was thrilled for her cousin. If anyone deserved it, Izzy did. And she'd been very generous with the family. But Charley didn't like taking handouts. She was going to make her way herself. And that meant she needed to get this damn job, which meant she needed to look fabulous.

She picked something and quickly slipped it on.

"I'm still not sure I feel totally right about this," she said, turning so Izzy could zip up the form-fitting black sheath dress.

Izzy sighed. "We've gone over this. Chris only went with your firm because I recommended *you*. Nothing has changed."

"Except that I'm no longer with my firm. Seems like something I should probably mention."

Izzy shrugged. "I don't see why. His office called you directly so he could work *with you*, and he is still working with you. What's the problem?"

"The problem is that his board was okay with his choice of a junior associate because of the firm behind me. Without that, I'm pretty sure they'd prefer to go with someone else."

"Well, they've already hired you, so I don't see how it matters. You'll still do an amazing job, they'll be happy, and you'll have a big-name client to get your business off the ground. It's not your fault your former company was full of misogynistic assholes who'd rather promote anyone with a penis over a woman, no matter how much more qualified she was. I see no reason to deprive Chris of the best person for the job just because your old boss was a shortsighted idiot who refused to give you the promotion you deserved."

Charley sighed. "I know, but maybe I should've sucked it up a few weeks longer. Until I'd finished with Mr. Lachlan's company. I'd still have gotten the credit, and then I could have gone out on my own without having to resort to this deception to do it."

Izzy snorted. "Seriously, Chuck, I'm not sure if your naivety is sweet or aggravating. Do you really think they'd have let you keep this account? If I hadn't given Chris your direct number and sent him through the firm instead, they'd have passed it off to someone else no matter who Chris requested. Probably that guy you spent a year training who they made your boss. They never appreciated you."

Charley grimaced, but she couldn't argue with that. Izzy was right. She shoved her feet into a pair of heels a good two inches higher than she normally wore and took a deep breath. "All right. How do I look?"

Izzy looked her over. "The clothes are perfect. Now let's do something about that," she said, waving her finger in Charley's face.

Right. Any bit of makeup she'd been wearing was now smeared all over her discarded bra. She grinned and shook her head but allowed Izzy to lead her to the vanity table filled with high-end beauty products.

Twenty minutes and thirty pounds of makeup later, Charley was ready for the meeting of her life. She just prayed her stomach didn't revolt. The last thing she needed was to make a total fool of herself in front of Chris Lachlan.

Chapter Two

Chris chugged the last of his protein shake and tossed the empty bottle to his assistant. Not surprisingly, she caught it without even breaking her stride.

The woman terrified him sometimes with her efficiency. But at the moment, he really wanted her to go away. Because if she reminded him of the damn insurance assessor guy one more time...

"And you're meeting with the representative from Phosphorus Assessments at one o'clock. The meeting location has been changed as you requested, and your reservations have been confir—"

"Zara."

He didn't need to say anything else. She knew the irritation behind those two syllables by now. Her face set in that stubborn look he dreaded, and she crossed her arms over the bundle of papers she held.

"Mr. Lachlan, your company's on the verge of going public and unless you want to wave good-bye to it as it takes off as the largest and most profitable vacation home rental company on the planet, you'll meet with the assessor so you can get insured and remain president."

He released a frustrated sigh. "I'm aware of all that. But..."

"No buts. If you miss this meeting, your board will have my head."

"Why? It wouldn't be your fault if I didn't show."

"With all due respect, sir, if you don't show, it will absolutely be my fault. And I'd like to keep my job."

She handed him a folder of info with a smile that somehow managed to be more stern than friendly, and he cocked an eyebrow at her.

"I promise, you'll keep your job," he said. "Though I'm not sure why you want it. I'm a nightmare."

That got him a genuine grin. "You have your moments, sir."

He took the folder and leafed through it. "What do we know about this guy?"

Zara shrugged. "Not much. Charley Claybourne is a junior assessor for the company, has worked there five years, and has a good track record with those he approves. Though he's a stickler for the rules and seems to have used an unusual number of sick and personal days. Even with that, he still gets his work in on time and by all accounts is dedicated to his job."

"If he's such a stickler, why did we go with him? Someone a little more lenient might have made this all go smoother."

"Possibly, but the board wanted a reputable firm so no one could question the results. Again. And Mr. Claybourne came highly recommended from Ms. Grenier."

"Ah yeah. The guy is Izzy's cousin or something, isn't he?"

"Yes, sir."

Chris sighed and gave the folder back to her. "Fine. I'll

meet with the guy, turn on the charm, be on my best behavior and all that until he signs off on me. Really," he said, heading for the bathroom in his office so he could change out of his workout clothes and into a suit, "everyone acts like I'm out swimming with sharks or something. I'm not that reckless."

"May I remind you that you *have* actually swam with sharks?"

Chris poked his head out so she could get the full effect of his eye roll. "Once."

"And the last two firms we approached with preliminary scenarios both reported they'd deny recommendation for insurance if hired due to your lifestyle."

That deserved another eye roll, but he kept it in and grabbed a tie. "Just because I like being hands-on and having some fun occasionally."

He stepped back into the office and caught Zara in mid-chuckle. She quickly shut it down, but her eyes still glistened with amusement. He gave her a mock glare and finished tying a perfect Windsor knot. The fact that he could do that without a mirror, or *at all*, would've made his teenage self want to junk punch him. Spending most of the day in a suit and skyscraper office was not the way he'd envisioned his life when he was younger. Or even when he'd started his company. He was grateful for his success. But it came with some definite downsides.

"I think some would find your version of amusement to be a bit…strenuous, sir."

"Only because those people can't imagine entertainment that actually takes place outside without a phone in their hands."

"Be that as it may, sir…"

He raised a hand to stop her. "I know, I know. I'll be on my best behavior, I promise."

She nodded and gave him an encouraging smile as he

headed out the door. He tugged on the tie strangling his neck and strode to the elevator. He wanted this meeting done and over with so he could get back to more important matters. Like stalking that convenience store until his milk-stealing beauty reappeared. He'd never been so intrigued by anyone in his life. She'd managed to amuse, frighten, and fascinate him all at once.

Well, at least the meeting with the assessor had been changed to his favorite restaurant instead of the conference room. If he had to kiss some ass, he'd rather do it with a good steak and better liquor than in the steel and glass coffin in the middle of his office building.

He just prayed the assessor wasn't a total drag.

He strode into his one o'clock meeting with a smile on his face, confident everything would go his way. Because it mostly always did.

And then he saw the woman sitting in his booth and stopped in his tracks.

It was *her*.

His irritation at the impending meeting evaporated, and he took advantage of the fact that she hadn't noticed him yet to take his time looking her over.

Auburn hair falling past her shoulders in soft waves. A flash of bright blue eyes as she looked nervously around the room. A black dress that hugged her in all the right ways. Sitting there in his booth like a delectable little treat someone had left him.

One he'd enjoy savoring if he ever got the chance.

She definitely cleaned up nice. Not that she hadn't been completely adorable earlier that day, even with flashing eyes and milk dripping off her.

But, of course, that left the question… What the ever-loving fuck was she doing there?

. . .

Charley glanced up at the person nearing the table she'd been seated at and nearly choked on her water.

Christopher Lachlan, in the flesh.

Again.

Looking much more put together than he had standing in that dairy section clutching her jug of milk. She *knew* he'd looked familiar. She should have recognized him, but it had never occurred to her that someone like him would be in a tiny store buying milk for himself. Plus, in every picture she'd ever seen of him, he'd been strutting the red carpet dressed to the nines or in a scuba mask or sunglasses or...something other than ratty workout clothes.

Oh, this couldn't be happening. She was unlucky. But come *on*. Who the hell did she piss off in a past life to deserve this level of payback?

She could only hope he wouldn't recognize her. It'd only been a few minutes. Hopefully he'd forgotten all about it and wouldn't connect the milk lady with the one in front of him now.

Here went nothing.

She stood up and offered her hand, taking a small step forward. A step that proved to be a huge mistake as her right heel had somehow snagged itself in the carpeting under the table. Her ankle rolled slightly, and a cracking sound emanated from the direction of her shoe.

Chris paused, his mouth open and eyes wide as they looked her over, lingering on her feet.

"Are you all right?" he asked.

She took a deep breath and forced a smile. "Fine. Thank you."

It wasn't fine. She was pretty sure her heel had just snapped. But at least it had been her shoe, not her ankle.

As long as they were sitting, it wouldn't be a problem. She'd solve the issue of how to get out of the restaurant without him seeing her hobble to the door on one shoe when the time came.

For the moment, she needed to greet her new client and make a good enough impression that he both didn't fire her and wouldn't remember the whole milk thing from earlier. She didn't have high hopes of success, but hey, a girl could dream.

She extended her hand again, grateful the damn thing wasn't shaking even though her insides had turned into a mosh pit.

"Mr. Lachlan," she said, giving him a firm, but not too firm, handshake. "It's a pleasure to meet you."

He gazed directly into her eyes, and she held her breath, wondering if he'd mention the milk incident. But after a few moments, he gave her a warm smile.

"Call me Chris, please. The pleasure is all mine." He gestured to her seat and had a seat himself. But he didn't take his eyes off her even for a second.

She sat, taking care to keep any weight off her broken right shoe as she did so. Thankfully, her butt hit the chair without further incident. Though Chris's intense scrutiny had her clasping her hands together in her lap, trying to resist the urge to squirm.

"I was expecting a *Mr.* Claybourne," he said. "Though I'm very pleased with the change in plans."

She tried to keep her expression neutral. "There's been no change, Mr. Lachlan. Chris," she amended when his eyebrow rose. "I'm Ms. Claybourne."

"Charley?" he said, his brow slightly furrowed.

Keep calm.

She gave him what she hoped was a soft, controlled smile. "Short for Charlotte-Leigh. Hyphenated so it's one name, not two. My parents couldn't decide which grandmother to name me after so chose them both."

His lips twitched, but he kept up the charming routine. "I like it. It's unusual."

She gave him her practiced smile again. "Yes, but extremely long. It never fits on forms, so a lot of places end up cutting it off somewhere in the middle. Which then leads the people reading those forms to think the name is supposed to be Charlie. Or Carl, occasionally, which never made sense to me. But in either case, it caused all sorts of fun problems, as you can imagine. Like freshman year of high school when I was given a locker in the boys' locker room because the administration just saw the Charl without checking my full name and assumed I was a boy."

His laughed bellowed out. "Nothing like making freshman year even more awkward."

A real smile slipped out this time. "Exactly. So, a shortened but more feminine nickname is usually the easiest way to go. Unless you're Izzy, who likes to shorten it even further."

"What's shorter than Charley?"

She hesitated, wishing her anxiety-induced word vomit hadn't made her spill this particular tidbit. He sat waiting, though, so she sighed. "Izzy tends to call me Chuck."

He laughed again, and she couldn't help but smile. Good God, the man went from a solid ten to an easy fifteen… *hundred* when he smiled. She was beginning to wish they'd done this whole meeting through email. She was nervous enough without having to deal with the most attractive man she'd ever met in her life. Her palms were sweating.

"I apologize for the confusion," she managed to say.

"Entirely my fault. My sincere apologies for my assumption," he said, putting his hand over his heart and giving her a little bow.

Well, things were already going better than she'd feared. They were chatting, enjoying themselves, and no mention of the fiasco earlier that day. Maybe he didn't realize Chocolate Milk Lady and she were one and the same. The waiter came over, and they ordered drinks. She ordered an iced tea. And he…

"I'll have an ice-cold chocolate milk," he said, looking straight at her. "Lactose-free if you have it."

Her jaw dropped. The waiter nodded and left to get their beverages.

"You *do* recognize me," she said, her composure slipping enough that it came out as more of a furious whisper than a statement.

He chuckled. "What happened this morning would be kind of hard to forget. Besides, you might be a bit more dressed up, but you still look like you. Definitely not a woman I'd forget." His eyes widened slightly at that remark, like he hadn't meant to let it slip out. "The incident was rather… memorable."

Yeah, hoping otherwise had probably been too optimistic. She sat back, her arms folded across her chest. "Why didn't you say something when you first arrived?"

He shrugged. "First of all, I was surprised to see you. I was expecting some middle-aged bald guy named Charlie, not a beautiful woman with the longest name in the world who likes to spend her spare time stealing milk from people in convenience stores."

She opened her mouth to refute that, while her stomach did a goofy little trip at the beautiful remark, but he plowed on ahead.

"And second of all, I didn't want to be rude. You seemed a little embarrassed when you left the store. I didn't think bringing it up when I first arrived for a business meeting was the right time or place."

Her eyes narrowed again. "Really? So, what's with the drink order then?"

"I'll have you know I really enjoy chocolate milk. It's incredibly delicious and refreshing, and I drink it a lot. And I didn't get any earlier today."

Her eyes narrowed further, and he grinned, sending her stomach acrobatics into overdrive. "And I couldn't resist."

"Uh huh." She let a long sigh out. Well, at least they'd gotten it out of the way. Maybe they could focus on more important things now.

The waiter returned, and she ordered a Caesar salad with grilled chicken. Chris, on the other hand, ordered a rare steak large enough to feed a family of four, baked potato with everything plus bacon, and broccoli casserole, which turned out to be a few bits of vegetables buried in butter, cheese, fried onions, and enough toasted breadcrumbs to choke a duck.

Her eyes widened when the food arrived, and he started chowing down.

"Eat like this a lot, do you?" she asked.

He shrugged. "I've got a great metabolism and exercise regularly." He patted what were probably rock-hard abs beneath his designer shirt. "So far I've been able to get away with it."

Hell yeah he had. She kept her lips firmly pinched together to keep that bit from slipping out, simply murmuring an, "Um hmm." She pulled out her tablet and entered a few codes onto the running spreadsheet she kept when assessing a client.

He tried to peer at it to see what she was doing. She didn't make any effort to hide it. He wouldn't be able to decipher what anything meant anyway.

"What's all that?" he asked, waving his fork at it.

"Part of your assessment."

"You're recording what I eat?"

"I record everything, Mr. Lachlan."

"Chris."

"Chris," she said, her cheeks heating. Crazy how one little syllable could seem so much more intimate. She would've preferred to keep calling him Mr. Lachlan. She needed something to help her keep some professional distance. She'd never wanted to lean across a table and lick a client before, but this one was sorely tempting her.

She gently cleared her throat. "It's how I can accurately assess the risk factors necessary to determine if I can recommend you for insurance or not."

He frowned at that. "I wasn't aware we'd start with the whole assessment thing so soon."

"I've actually almost completed my assessment of you, Mr...Chris. Meeting you is the last step, not the first."

"How do you assess someone you've never met?"

She allowed a small smile to peek through. This was one of her favorite subjects. "You're a public figure. Quite a bit of information about your lifestyle is available through a number of different social media sites and publications."

He put his fork down and sat back in his chair. "Information such as?"

"Hobbies, activities, sports, dating habits. Your Instagram account is a fairly detailed account of your life."

"Is it really?" he asked, his voice low and quiet.

She frowned a little. "You don't seem to be very happy with my answers."

"Do you blame me?"

She shrugged. "I'm confused by your response. You're the one who posts everything. From that one account alone, I know you're a borderline adrenaline junkie who enjoys activities like skydiving, scuba diving, zip lining, surfing, hiking, white water rafting, and a number of more questionable past times. You spend most of your time traveling around—"

"And traveling a lot is a crime?"

"Of course not, but it's a risk. There's no need for you to visit your properties yourself. You have more than enough employees who could do that kind of thing for you."

"I like keeping tabs on how everything is doing. In person."

"Which is understandable and admirable. But again, it's a risk factor, and I have to take that into consideration. Like it or not, everything you do, everything you eat, the steady stream of women from all over the world you date, except for the year you dated Cass—"

His face hardened further, if possible, at the mention of Cass's name. "I don't see how my dating life is at all relevant."

Charley squirmed a little under his gaze, more than a little uncomfortable at this particular line of conversation. But she pressed on. "Well, according to available sources, you once dated a suspected cartel princess, another woman who was a known jewel thief, and another one who was arrested for espionage."

He waved that away. "Svetlana isn't a spy. That was just a misunderstanding. And nothing bad has ever happened during my travels or because of the women I date. Everything always works out just fine."

She nodded. He wasn't wrong. He hadn't earned the nickname Golden Boy for nothing. Still...

"Sure. So far. But my job is to assess future risk and I'm afraid—"

"I don't know what you think you know about me, but scrolling through a bunch of pictures doesn't tell you a damn thing about who I really am."

She put her own fork down and sat back. "It does tell me about the life you live, but I agree, it doesn't tell me anything about who you are as a person. Which is why I like to meet my clients face to face. Though, to be honest, it's not necessary. My job is to assess the risk to an insurance company should they choose to insure you. You're worth quite a bit, Mr. Lachlan. Should something happen to you, an insurance company would have to pay out quite a large sum of money. And in order to assess that risk, all most companies want to know is what the likelihood is that they'll have to write out a fat check. Most of them would have seen the pictures of you surrounded by sharks in Bora Bora and would have stamped a big red DENY on your folder and moved on. I like to take a closer look."

His eyebrows went up at that. "And what is that closer look telling you so far?"

She glanced at the heart attack on a plate in front of him and debated whether or not to tell him the truth. Most men in his position didn't like to be told they were in the wrong, no matter the situation. But she'd never let that stop her before, and she wasn't going to start now. "It's not helping much, I'm afraid."

To her surprise, he grinned. But before he could say anything, someone interrupted.

"Well, this is a surprise!"

Charley looked up to see Izzy standing by their table. Chris stood and gave her a quick hug and kiss on the cheek.

"What are you guys doing here?" she asked. She grabbed a chair from the next table and sat down with them. "I thought your big meeting was at your office."

"I thought this would be more comfortable and personal. And I was hungry," he said.

Izzy snorted. "As always. So," she said, glancing between them. "How's it going?"

"I believe she was about to tell me I'm too big a risk to recommend," he said, pinning Charley with an accusing gaze.

Izzy looked over at her, obviously surprised. "But you've

only just met him."

"Yes, but apparently I've been damned by Instagram," he said. "But at least she got it over with quickly instead of dragging it out for months. So," he stood up, "as we seem to be finished, I believe I'll excuse myself. I've got a trip to pack for."

Charley sucked in a breath and made a slight gasping sound that she immediately clamped her lips on. After all, it wasn't surprising he was upset. Explaining she hadn't totally finished her assessment wouldn't help matters, though, since it *was* likely she wouldn't recommend him as he rightly assumed. So, she just kept her mouth shut and ignored the sinking feeling in her gut.

Izzy, however, didn't seem to share her fatalistic attitude. "Wait a second," she said. "Come on, Chris. Sit down."

He sighed but did as requested. "Now come on you two, I'm sure something can be worked out. Charley, I've known him for years. He's a good man. Yes, he has some questionable habits," she said, giving him the side-eye when he snorted. "But he's worked his ass off to get where he is. Surely you could take a deeper look."

Charley opened her mouth to say that it would be a waste of time, but the glimmering bit of hope in his eyes stopped her. Good God. The man could get away with murder with puppy dog eyes like those.

"I suppose…"

"Excellent," Izzy said, not letting her finish. "I've just had an amazing idea. You're getting ready to go on another trip to check on some of your properties, right?" she asked him.

He frowned. "Yes. There are a few I haven't been to in quite a while. There have been an unusual number of repairs on some lately, and nothing but glowing reports on others. I need to see what's going on."

"Glowing reports are bad?" Charley asked.

"If that's all I ever get, sure. Properties need maintenance. If I have a property that never needs anything fixed, it usually means my property manager isn't doing his job."

"And too many reports means…"

"That the property manager might be inflating reports to pocket the money I'm shelling out for repairs."

Charley nodded. She hadn't thought about any of that stuff. Intriguing.

Izzy ignored that little exchange and pressed on with her own questions. "Okay. And you think these trips are unnecessary and risky, correct?" she asked, looking at Charley.

"Yes," Charley answered, drawing the word out. Both because she wasn't sure she still believed that based on what Chris had just said. And because she had a feeling she knew where this was going, and she didn't like it. Neither did Chris, who was focusing that intense gaze of his at Izzy.

"So, why don't you go on the trip with him?"

He and Charley both started to protest, but Izzy waved all that away. "It's the perfect solution. Chris can check on his properties, and you can see what really happens on these trips of his and see that there's no unusual risk that should keep you from recommending him."

She glanced back and forth between them. Chris scowled, but he finally sighed. "I guess it's better than you judging me based on a bunch of pictures."

Izzy nodded. "There. It's all settled."

"I'm not sure this is appropriate," Charley said. "Going on an extravagant trip with a client could be seen as bribery." She glanced at him and the enticing temptation he was lounging in his perfectly tailored suit that made long-dormant parts of her want to sit up and scream *hello*. "Or worse."

Izzy waved that away. "It's a perfectly legit business trip. Nobody'll think anything."

"I'm not so sure…" Charley tried to protest, but Izzy totally ignored her.

"Lighten up, Chuckles. It'll be fun." Then she turned to Chris. "Just give me a date and time and I'll make sure she's there."

"Fine. But pack light," he said, standing up again. He turned to leave but then glanced back at her over his shoulder. "And don't forget your chocolate milk."

Chapter Three

Chris threw down another winning hand, and his fellow poker players groaned. He grinned and dragged the large pile of chips toward him.

"We really need to stop letting him play," Brooks said. "Or give him a handicap or something."

Chris snorted. "Not my fault you play like shit. Gotta get your head back in the game."

"Easier said than done when there's so much to distract me," he said, giving his wife a look that was probably melting the panties right off her. Leah blushed but gave Brooks a smile that made Chris's heart ache with a twinge of jealousy for a second.

He pushed the feeling away. He was happy for his friends. Thrilled. And it wasn't that he wanted to join them in wedded bliss or anything. He was quite happy being the confirmed bachelor of the group. But he did feel like the lonely third wheel more often than not lately. Or...seventh wheel, as the case might be.

Harrison chuckled. "Don't blame Chris. You're the one

who suggested we let the wives play."

Brooks scowled at him but picked up Leah's hand to give it a kiss. "Sure, but I didn't think anyone would agree."

Leah rolled her eyes and pushed him away. "We don't join you often. Believe it or not, we girls like our nights out without you, too."

Brooks clapped his hand over his heart like he'd been shot and mock gasped. Leah rolled her eyes while the rest of the group laughed.

Harrison gathered up the cards and started shuffling them. "What do you ladies do when you're off without us, anyway? Nicole didn't make it home until sunrise the last time you went out."

Kiersten, Leah, and Nikki all looked at one another, then everywhere but at one another, which made all the men sit back with interest. Chris watched, silently chuckling at his friends' reactions to their wives' guilty faces. Until those guilty faces glanced his way.

"What?" he asked.

Kiersten cleared her throat. "It's nothing much. We had dinner and then headed to the theater, and while we were there, we ran into Izzy and...Cass..." Again, her gaze darted to him and then quickly away. She shrugged. "She's getting ready to open a new art gallery and offered to show it to us, so we went with her afterward, and some other friends were invited along the way, and it sort of turned into a thing."

"A thing?" Cole asked, eyebrow cocked. "And were there handsome men at this *thing*?" His face was stern, but his tone was teasing. He knew he had nothing to worry about. Kiersten was head over heels for him and had been since the day she'd won the lottery and started torturing him as payback for being such a crappy boss.

Kiersten smiled at her husband. "Just a few friends of Cass's boyfriend. But none near so handsome as you," she said, leaning over to give him a kiss before realizing what she'd let slip.

She looked over at Chris, her mouth slightly open, but he waved her off.

"It's okay. We've been broken up for over a year. She's entitled to date who she wants."

"Well, if helps, I don't think they're dating anymore."

Chris shrugged. "Not my business."

Cole took a drink of his beer and then nodded at Chris. "You ever going to tell us why you two broke up? You were good together."

Chris shrugged again, not wanting to have this conversation. Then again, with as involved as his friends were in his life, it was a miracle he'd been able to put it off this long.

He picked up the cards Harrison had dealt him and shuffled them back and forth. "There's nothing much to tell. We wanted different things."

"Like what?" Brooks asked.

Chris sighed. "I don't think either of us knew. We just knew the other person wasn't it."

His friends sat silent, obviously not sure how to respond.

"It's not a big deal, guys," he said, trying to lighten the mood. "Cass is great. I cared about her a lot. Still do. But at the end of the day, I think we were looking for something the other person didn't have. It was a mutual breakup, no hard feelings. You guys don't have to walk on eggshells around the subject or avoid mentioning her. I know you're still friends," he said, nodding at Kiersten and the other women.

Kiersten gave him a maternal smile, which amused him considering he was older than her. "Well," she said, patting his hand, "I hope you find whatever it is you're looking for."

He took her hand and gave it a quick kiss. "Me too," he said with a rush of warm affection. "I promise, I'm good." And he was happy to realize he meant it. Cass had been great. But they hadn't been right for each other, and he was good with how things ended. "Now, are we going to play or what? I've got a trip to pack for."

Cole and Harrison folded while the rest of the group threw in their chips and traded in cards.

"Yeah, Izzy mentioned you were headed out again," Kiersten said, not bothering to hide her grin.

He scowled. "Izzy and I are going to have to have a serious talk next time I see her."

Brooks leaned forward like a bloodhound who'd just caught a whiff of steak. "Well, this sounds juicy. Spill it, bro."

Chris glared at him. "She's saddled me with the risk assessor who's about to flunk me right out of my business."

The ladies all had varying degrees of guilty and amused smirks on their faces and were obviously avoiding looking at him.

"Uh huh, and what's the rest of the story?" Harrison asked. When no one answered, he grabbed his wife and pulled her to his lap. "Spill it, Nikki," he said, rubbing the scruff of his new beard on her neck until she squealed.

"Okay, okay!"

He stopped long enough for her to catch her breath.

"The risk assessor is a gorgeous woman named Charley. She's sweet, funny, wicked smart, and Izzy said Chris couldn't take his eyes off her during their meeting."

Chris frowned at her. "How would Izzy know? And who told you?"

Leah chimed in again. "Izzy filled us in. And Charley was at the gallery opening, so we've already met her." She turned to her husband. "She's adorable. I can totally see what Chris sees in her."

Brooks turned a delighted grin his way, but Chris held his hand up. "I don't see anything in her. She's a pain in my ass, and she's only coming with me because of Izzy."

"Maybe, but those pains in the ass tend to grow on you," Cole said, winking at Kiersten. She swatted at him, but the love shining from her face gave Chris another slight jealous twinge he didn't want to examine too closely.

"You're all a pain in my ass," he grumbled. "And Ms. Claybourne is off-limits, no matter how 'adorable' she may be."

"Why?" Harrison asked.

"Because the last thing in the world I need is to give the insurance company any more reasons to deny coverage. If there's even a rumor that something may have happened between me and the assessor, that's all the reason they'll need to decide her assessment was coerced or bribed and I'm screwed. Even if I was interested in her, and I'm not, she's so far off-limits she might as well be on a different planet."

His friends exchanged disappointed looks that still held an unhealthy amount of smug speculation. They were impossible. Hell, even if what he was saying wasn't true, she'd probably never believe he was interested in her because he genuinely liked her. He'd certainly had his fair share of women throwing themselves at him because they wanted something from him. He'd never been in the position to return the favor, but he had no trouble seeing how the intriguing Charley Claybourne might assume he was only interested in her in order to get a good assessment out of her. True or not, it would be an understandable assumption on her part. And not one he could easily refute. He'd never use her like that, but he *did* want a good assessment.

Which made the entire situation impossible and pointless to keep thinking about.

He dropped his cards and pushed away from the table. "I fold. And I've got to go. Leaving early in the morning."

He downed the rest of his whisky and ignored the good-natured jokes his friends lobbed at him as he left Cole and

Kiersten's apartment.

He normally enjoyed his business trips. Traveling all over the world, enjoying everything each new place had to offer. What wasn't to like? Only this time he'd be second-guessing every move he made. It kind of felt like being at a chaperoned dance. Who could have fun with someone always looking over their shoulder?

Then again, Charley was nothing like the chaperones at his grade schools. She might look like she was all business, but there was a fire behind her eyes begging to be stoked.

He just wouldn't be able to do the stoking.

Still, he caught a smile playing on his lips in his reflection on the shiny elevator doors and looked up to avoid seeing himself. Thankfully, none of his friends were there to see it. Because like it or not, he was almost looking forward to this trip.

Almost.

Chapter Four

Charley climbed out of the taxi Izzy had shoved her into and stared into the plane hangar.

Three planes occupied the huge space. One of those little prop engine planes, one that looked like what she'd always envisioned a billionaire's private plane to look like—smooth, sleek, and big enough to carry an entourage. But the one with the engines revving and all the people scurrying around it was a much smaller version.

A man in a suit hurried over to her, his hand out to take her bag. "Ms. Claybourne?"

She nodded, still staring at the plane where she was pretty sure Chris had just taken a seat.

"I'm Lucas, Mr. Lachlan's head of security. He asked me to get you aboard and settled."

"And where is Mr. Lachlan?" she asked, afraid she already knew the answer.

"In the cockpit getting the plane ready."

"But…" she started, but Lucas put a firm hand on her back and led her toward the plane.

The interior was gorgeous, of course. All pale leather and wood. The cushy-looking seats looked more like expensive leather recliners than airline seats. There was only space for about seven passengers. Up front on the left were two plush seats facing each other opposite a couch on the right, which would comfortably seat three. Behind them were two more seats, one on either side of a narrow doorway she assumed led to the bathroom. It looked more like a lux SUV than a friggin' plane.

"You decided to come after all," Chris said.

He was in the pilot's seat, looking over his shoulder at her. She could only glance at him, back at the rest of the plane, then back at him again.

He laughed. "Come on. You can sit up here with me if you want."

Uh, no. That wasn't what she wanted. What she wanted was to be in a nice big plane that had enough space that she could at least pretend she was on a train or something. Not this little sardine can of a flying machine.

Then again, if she had to fly on this thing, she'd rather not do it sitting all by herself. Maybe being able to watch out the front window would help.

"You can stow your carry-on in that closet there," he said, pointing to a narrow wood panel opposite the door that popped open when she pushed on it.

"Is that all the luggage you brought?"

She nodded. "My luggage tends to go missing when I travel. So I only bring what I can carry. It's easier to buy what I might need once I get there."

She got her bag stashed and then climbed into the seat beside Mr. Lachlan, her eyes darting across the massive dashboard full of blinking lights and gauges.

"Do you like it?" he asked, his gesture taking in the plane. The pride in his voice made her loathe to say anything unflattering. And really, if she hadn't been moments from hurtling through the air in the thing, she'd be enjoying the experience much more. Even the cockpit seats were more comfortable than her couch at home.

"It's beautiful," she said, glancing around again. "But… why aren't we taking one of the bigger planes?"

"There's only the two of us. We don't need that many seats."

"Right. Okay. But…shouldn't somebody else be flying?"

Chris shrugged. "Why pay money for a pilot when I'm capable of doing it myself? Besides, I enjoy flying, and I don't get to do it as often as I'd like."

She quickly typed a note into her tablet. He rolled his eyes, and she turned the tablet away so he couldn't see what she was writing.

He snorted and kept flipping switches and checking panels. "You know, statistically speaking, you're safer flying than driving in a car. And we're much safer with me flying than relying on someone else. I'm trained, licensed, and experienced. I also know for a fact I'm sober and well rested. The same cannot be said for whatever random pilot might happen to be flying another plane we could get on."

Charley thought about that for a second and hated that it sounded so reasonable. "Okay," she said, "but aren't these little planes more susceptible to crashing than the larger ones? Every time you hear about some celebrity crashing, it's in some tiny plane."

"That doesn't have anything to do with the plane or its safety. I bet you hear more about celebrity car accidents than other car accidents, too. That doesn't make cars less safe or keep you from operating one, does it?"

"No." She frowned. No way would she win this argument if he kept bringing logic into it.

"Besides, these babies are actually quite a bit safer. We

don't fly as high, there's less luggage and passengers and therefore less possibility of passenger interference, and a whole bunch of other statistics that I could spout at you but won't. I'm trying to keep my company here. Do you think I'd purposely do something I considered dangerous when I know you're going to be sitting there judging my every move?"

"No. I guess not. And I'm not judging your every move."

"Uh huh."

She ignored that but narrowed her eyes and stared at him for a moment, trying to gauge how truthful he was being about the plane. But again, she had to admit he sounded pretty reasonable. She'd have to do some research and look into the true statistics. She jotted down another note in her tablet.

"Are you going to be messing with that thing the entire trip?"

"Yes. That's kind of the point of the whole trip, isn't it?" she asked. "I'm here to watch what you usually do and assess how risky your behavior is."

He shook his head and turned his attention back to the plane. "Well, I can't imagine we're off to a good start when you've already made six notes in your tablet and we haven't even left the hangar yet."

She couldn't help but grin at that. "Don't worry about it. They aren't all bad. I promise I'll be fair."

"If you say so." He flipped a few more switches and then spoke to someone over the headphones he was wearing, instructing them that he was ready and to close the door.

"What?" he asked, his eyes wide with what looked like first shock, then irritation. "You have got to be kidding me," he grumbled, unbuckling his seat belt and striding out of the cockpit and then the plane.

"What are you all doing here?" she could hear him ask. There were some responses she couldn't quite catch. Then a,

"You are *not* coming..." from Chris.

And then feet, many feet, quickly moving up the few steps into the plane. Charley climbed out of her seat and stood in the cockpit doorway to see what was going on.

"Hi there, Charley! Nice to see you again." The bubbly brunette with black-rimmed glasses she'd met at Cass's party boarded the plane with a huge grin.

"Hi...Nikki," she said, glad to have remembered the woman's name but completely at a loss as to why she was there.

She didn't have too long to wonder, though, because Leah, Kiersten, and Izzy were right behind her. She greeted them all as they boarded and found a seat, trying to look over their shoulders at the men whose voices were raised but indistinguishable. She finally gave up and turned back to the women.

"Are you all coming with us?"

"Not for the whole trip, just the first leg," Izzy said. "Cass is opening a mini-hotel in Costa Rica in a few weeks, and since you guys are headed there first, we figured we'd hitch a ride."

"Oh. That's convenient," Charley said with a smile, relieved, and slightly disappointed, she wouldn't be alone with Chris. She ignored the disappointment. Was it fun to be going on a trip with a hot billionaire? Sure. Mostly. Okay, it was a bit intimidating but still, once in a lifetime, right?

But—and this was a big but—this was a business trip. And things needed to stay businesslike. Something she could see getting out of hand far too easily. Well, if he didn't totally resent her for her very existence and if she could figure out how to just have fun for once in her life. All moot points as this was a business trip. Any hint of anything going on between her and Chris and her career was over.

She was a woman in a mostly male industry. Any time

she even glanced at a man in a senior position for a fraction of a second too long, she was accused of trying to use her body to gain a leg up. Pun totally intended. Now she was trying to start her own business, and not being totally honest with her first client was already a strike against her. Getting involved with him in any personal capacity would be the kiss of death. She'd always be known as the chick who slept with her clients to get ahead. No way was she going to let that happen, no matter how much her neglected hormones perked up every time he was close to her.

The presence of her cousin and his friends would help her keep that straight in her head. Hopefully. She didn't like the speculative gleam in their eyes when Chris re-boarded, gave them all a good grimace, and headed back to the cockpit.

Before she could say anything, the rest of the men entered. They introduced themselves in short order, each shaking her hand and looking her over the way her father used to look over her dates, before going to sit with their wives. Izzy sat on the couch with Cole and Kiersten while Brooks and Leah took the two seats up front, and Harrison and Nikki took the two in back. Which meant Charley had nowhere to go but back in the cockpit.

"Ms. Claybourne!" Mr. Lachlan said, summoning her from the front. "Let's go!"

She gave her audience a smile and then retook her seat next to Chris, who handed her a pair of headphones. He didn't look happy.

"I guess you weren't expecting them?" she asked.

"No, but I probably should've been."

She glanced at him with a frown, confused, but he shook his head. "Never mind. Let's just say my friends need to work on their boundaries."

Yeah, she got that, especially since Izzy was a pain in the ass they shared.

He turned his attention back to the plane while the crew outside got them sealed up and ready to go. He seemed to relax a little as he concentrated on what he was doing, and she realized the tension tightening a knot in her shoulders eased up as he did.

"Here we go," he said, edging the plane out of the hangar and slowly out onto the runway.

She cinched her seat belt and held onto it as if that would somehow help if the plane fell out of the sky.

"You might want to stow that tablet somewhere," he said. "If we crash, it'll just become a projectile."

She sucked in a breath, her eyes darting over to his. She tried to keep her face neutral but knew she failed when he started chuckling.

"Relax," he said. "I'm teasing. I mean, I'm not. It's true. But you don't need to worry about it. We'll be fine."

"Uh huh," she said and turned her attention back out the window. She knew the motor beneath them was a lot less powerful than the ones in the big jets that she usually flew in, but for some reason, the rumble of the building power felt a whole lot worse. Maybe because this time she was sitting right on top of it.

He leaned over and straightened out her seat belt, his fingers grazing against her hip when he tugged. The movement had her sucking in a breath. A motion that had her drowning in his intoxicating scent. It reminded her of clean laundry and something…spicy. He was close enough that if she sat forward ever-so-slightly, she'd be able to press her lips to that delicious spot right where his neck met his broad shoulders.

"There," he said, glancing up at her but not moving away. "Now you're all safe and secure."

"Thanks," she said, though the word was barely more than a whisper. She licked her suddenly dry lips and then forgot how to breathe when his gaze zeroed in on her mouth.

"Hey, Chris," one of the guys called from the back. "What's with the tiny plane?"

Chris closed his eyes for a second, like he was trying to get a grip on himself, and then scowled and sat back. She sucked in a ragged breath, understanding the feeling completely. What the hell had *that* been? The man got within a few inches and barely touched her, and she'd been ready to throw her career out the window and go all vampire on him. She seriously needed to rein it in.

Business trip, business trip, business trip, she repeated to herself over and over in her head.

"Yeah," another voice—Brooks?—said. "Why aren't we taking one of the bigger planes?"

Chris redid his own seat belt. "Because I wasn't expecting a plane full of passengers," he called over his shoulder. "If you're uncomfortable, you're welcome to hop out. I might even slow down first."

His tone was irritated, but his lips twitched when a chorus of laughter followed his suggestion. She hadn't been sure about his friends joining them when they'd first shown up. The trip was awkward enough without seven people watching them like they were the hottest show in town. But their presence also took a little pressure off her. Being comfortable alone with a guy like Christopher Lachlan was definitely something that was going to take getting used to and having the friend buffer was kind of nice. Plus, it meant his attention wasn't 100 percent focused on her the whole time. That would make assessing him easier. He was already twitchy every time she so much as glanced at her tablet.

"They have a point," she said. "If we're going to be in this tiny little thing, we might as well have taken that little crop duster you had sitting in there."

"That would have solved our unexpected passenger problem," he said. "But that plane doesn't have a big enough fuel tank to get us to where we need to go."

"And this one does?"

He shrugged. "It should get us most of the way there."

The blood left her face in a rush that made her dizzy, and his laughter filled the cockpit. "Oh my God, you really need to relax. It's just a plane. It's perfectly safe. It's constantly inspected and maintained. In fact, I guarantee you this plane is better inspected, better maintained, and piloted by someone with more experience and a better record than any of the planes you'd climb on in a commercial airport. My goal isn't to pack in as many people as cheaply as possible to make a buck. My goal is to get us where we need to go safely. Just sit back and enjoy the ride."

She released a deep breath, somewhat comforted by his logic. So, she sat back, determined to chill as much as possible. But there was no way in hell she was going to *enjoy* the ride. Flying wasn't her favorite thing to do anyway, but at least on a commercial airline the airplane was big enough that she could fool herself into believing she was anywhere else except hurtling through space with hardly anything between her and the huge sky.

The plane picked up speed and launched into the sky with a bump that had her pressing back into her seat, though she tried to keep her face neutral.

"Want to hold my hand?" he asked with a laugh, holding it out to her.

Yes, she did. She really, really did. But she shook her head. "No, thanks."

"Probably best. I kind of need it to fly."

She gave him as much of a smile as she could muster. He winked at her, turning her insides to mush for an entirely different reason, and then turned his attention back to the horizon.

She took a deep breath, determined to maintain her

composure even if it killed her. Not that losing it would kill her. A tiny little toy plane falling from the sky was probably going to kill her. But screaming like a maniac wouldn't make that circumstance any better.

Once they'd left the ground, though, her death grip on her seat belt loosened a bit as her attention was drawn to the scenery spreading out before her. In the larger planes she'd flown in, she'd seen the ground getting further away, of course, as the plane ascended. But she'd never seen it from the front of the plane. Never been just a pane of glass away from the sky that they were currently slicing through. It was an all-together different experience, one that fascinated her enough it pushed her fear aside. A bit, anyway. They went through some low-lying clouds, and she sucked in a breath at the wispy whiteness that floated past their windows before disappearing as the sky once again filled her vision.

She sighed, more in awe than fear, leaning forward a little so she could look out from all the windows.

"It's beautiful, isn't it?" Chris asked, his gaze laser-focused on her.

She glanced at him, but the intensity of his expression, and the fact that he was looking at her, not out the window, had her quickly averting her eyes back to the window. "It really is. Everything looks so small from up here. Like we're looking down at a toy landscape or something."

He laughed. "It does."

"I mean, I've been in planes before, and it always looks like that. But, in this plane, it just seems...I don't know... closer."

"Well, it is. Technically." He gestured out the window. "In a larger plane, you have a good deal more plane between you and the sky. It's why I like flying myself in these smaller planes. Feels more like I'm actually soaring through the air and less like I'm in some overstuffed, earthbound train."

She nodded, understanding the feeling completely.

"It's not so bad, is it?" he asked, with a smug but friendly smile.

She smiled back. "No. Not so bad." She glanced back out the window. "So far, anyway."

He laughed at that. "You're hard to impress, aren't you?"

"I don't think so." She looked back at him. "Are you trying to impress me?"

He frowned a little, his forehead creasing with slight look of confusion. "I was going to say no, but you know what? I might be."

Her eyes widened. "That's not something most guys would admit to."

He shrugged. "I'm not most guys."

Her lips twitched at that, agreeing wholeheartedly, but she refrained from commenting. Things were getting far too friendly in the small cabin. Time to get things back on track. She grabbed her messenger bag from beneath her seat, but the strap stuck on something. Figured. She gave it a good tug, and it came undone with a jerk that had her arm flinging to the side. Right into a control panel.

An alarm immediately sounded, and she shrank back against her seat in a rush of horror.

"Oh my God, I'm so sorry! What did I do?" she asked, trying to keep it under control but quickly losing her grip in the flood of terror pounding through her.

Chris flipped a few switches, his initial shock giving way to an amused chuckle. "It's fine, you just bumped one of the sensors. We aren't going to die."

She slapped a hand over her chest, trying to keep her heart from jumping out of her chest. "Gee, that makes me feel so much better."

He grinned at her again, and her lips twitched into a smile before she could stop it. She didn't know what the man was doing running a company for vacation homes. He should be on the covers of magazines with that billion-watt smile.

She took a deep breath, trying to collect herself into some semblance of professional composure, and pulled her tablet out from the pocket where she'd stowed it.

Chris saw it and scowled. "I guess it was too much to hope that you would go more than ten minutes before pulling that thing out again."

"It *is* why I'm here."

"True. But that doesn't mean you can't relax and just enjoy the trip now and then."

"I prefer to keep focused on the task at hand."

"Yeah, I can tell."

She frowned at that. "What do you mean?"

He shrugged, his gaze on the window. "You seem like the type that always has it all under control, you know. Or at least tries to. Yet even with all that effort, you still seem to be one second away from total disaster. I can't tell if you know it's coming or if you're just prepared in case something does happen, but...and I mean no offense by this...you'd make a hyperactive squirrel on crack nervous."

That startled a choked laugh out of her. She wanted to be offended, but man, he had her pegged, all right.

"Let's just say I have enough experience in dealing with disasters that I assume they're always looming, and I like to be prepared."

He cocked an eyebrow at that. "Sounds like you've got a few interesting stories."

She snorted. "You have no idea."

Before he could respond to that, someone piped up from the back again.

"Hey, Captain, are we free to move about the cabin yet?"

Chris scowled and grabbed the small intercom handset from the dashboard. "Attention, travelers. On behalf of

Lachlan Airlines, I'd like to say you're all going to hell for choosing our airline today. We know you have a choice when you travel and really wish you'd chosen any, and I mean ANY, other airline. As a special treat, you will be confined to your seats for the duration of the flight. All talking to the captain is strictly prohibited. Thank you and have a miserable day."

Howls and boos echoed through the small cabin, and Charley laughed then shook her head. "You can't keep them tied down the whole trip."

Chris sighed. "I know, but it's worth a try."

Brooks jutted his head into the cockpit, and Charley jumped in her seat with a stifled scream.

"Sorry, didn't mean to scare you," he said, smiling down at her. Then he looked over at Chris. "We all took off our seat belts and are moving about the cabin willy-nilly, despite your instructions. Got any peanuts or anything up here?"

He leaned in and started rooting through the pockets and small spaces in the cockpit while Chris tried to shoo him away. Not that it did any good. Chris finally took a magazine from the bin by his side and smacked Brooks over the head with it.

"Get out of here, you giant pain in the ass!"

Brooks fended him off, laughing as he backed away. Then he shoved his head back, this time looking at Charley. "He's abusive. Write that down," he said, pointing at her tablet before dodging Chris's magazine again and fleeing back to his seat.

"Your friends are quite the group," Charley said with a grin.

"Ha! You have no idea."

The flight attendant's light buzzed, and he groaned.

"There's food in the cabinet," he called back over his shoulder. "Now be quiet so I can concentrate on not killing us."

A chorus of "ooo"s erupted from the back. Charley's stomach dropped at Chris's comment, though she was fairly sure he was joking. She shifted a bit in her seat.

"I'm just messing with them," he said. "I've got the plane on auto right now."

She shifted a bit more. "Is that safe?"

"Completely."

She nodded, though it would take a little more convincing to keep her colon from twisting into knots.

"Relax," he said, reaching over to pat her hand. It took more willpower than she wanted to admit to keep from grabbing hold of it and squeezing for all she was worth. She really needed to work on the whole fear of flying thing.

"You don't fly much, do you?" he asked.

"Not if I can help it."

He shook his head. "I get it, I guess. But I could never give up these views." He gestured to the panoramic glory spread out before them.

"It's gorgeous, but I'm not really a fan of modes of transportation where I'm not in control."

"Ahh, a control freak, eh?"

She scowled at that. "Just because someone likes to be in control of a situation doesn't make them a freak."

He held up his hands. "Just an expression."

She released her breath slowly, concentrating on controlling her breathing until her body relaxed. "I know. Sorry."

He opened his mouth to respond when the flight attendant light buzzed again.

"When do we get drink service?"

Chris rubbed his hand over his face. "If I throw them all out of the plane without parachutes, will that reflect negatively on that spreadsheet of yours?"

She couldn't help but smile at that. "Probably."

"Shame." He unstrapped and climbed from his seat, but he paused to lean over her before heading back to deal with his friends.

"The plane is on auto. We're perfectly safe. Try not to have a panic attack until I get back." He gave her a wink that had her squirming like an 8th grader at her first co-ed dance. She tried to cover by rolling her eyes, but he laughed and headed to the cabin.

"Get a grip," she muttered to herself.

It was going to be a long, long trip.

Chapter Five

Chris landed the plane with a practiced smoothness that filled him with pride and slowly taxied it to the small hangar where it'd be stored while they were in Costa Rica.

His friends were already gathering their things and exiting the plane, the boys stopping to throw flirtatious looks at Charley while the women gave her friendly smiles and tried to herd their husbands out the door. He had no clue what they all thought they were doing, but he was going to kill them all for it anyway.

Yes, it was true Cass had her hotel opening soon, and it was plausible they'd all been invited for a soft opening as Harrison had done when he'd opened his family's castle to visitors the year before. Chris wouldn't know, because if that was the case, Cass hadn't invited him.

At least he wouldn't have to worry about dealing with an ex in front of Charley...

He stepped from the plane and stopped short. Speak of the devil.

Charley bumped into him from behind and muttered an

apology as she bent to pick up the bags she'd dropped. He shook his head and leaned down to help her, trying to keep from laughing. The woman was a walking menace. Assessing risk for a living was probably the perfect job for her. She'd need to know the exact risk of any given situation so she'd know her probability of making it out alive.

The brief respite of helping her momentarily erased Cass from his mind. But it didn't last. He stood up to find himself face to face with her.

"Hello, Chris," she said, a hesitant smile on her lips.

He took in the face that he'd once thought he'd wake up to for the rest of his life and nodded. Polite, though not quite friendly. He wasn't sure what to expect from her.

"I'm Cass Coy," she said, turning to Charley with an outstretched hand.

"Charley Claybourne, pleased to meet you," Charley responded, though her gaze flicked briefly to his as she shook Cass's hand.

"I didn't realize you'd be flying everyone in," Cass said, turning back to him.

"Neither did I," he muttered, shooting his friends a glare.

Cass laughed, and Chris relaxed a bit. "Yeah, that sounds about right. Well, I don't know what your plans are while you're here," she said, glancing between him and Charley. "But you're both welcome to stay at my hotel. I have another suite available that I can have made ready in no time."

Chris blinked at the realization that Cass thought Charley was there with him. "Oh…we're not here together. I mean, she did come with me but only under duress, not romantic circumstances. Not that she's here under duress, but…ah hell."

Cass's eyes widened, and she bit her lip, obviously trying to keep from laughing. Charley just watched him with a slight hint of confusion. He needed to get a grip. Although considering he just got blindsided by his ex in front of the woman on whom his career hung and their gaggle of boundary-deficient friends, it really wasn't going all that bad.

Cass's gaze switched to Charley, and she gave a gentle shake of her head, her lips twitching again. Chris glanced at her as well, wondering what was so amusing. Charley was the picture of elegant poise…until he noticed she'd managed to kick her shoe off and was trying to slide her foot back into it without being noticed. Only her toes kept missing it.

He took pity and nudged it in her direction. Her strained smile turned more genuine as her foot slipped into her sandal. "I'm here to evaluate Mr. Lachlan as part of his risk assessment," she said in that smooth, quiet tone of hers. "For his insurance application. Sharing a suite would be…"

"Oh," Cass said, surprise in her voice. "I understand. I'm afraid I only have the one suite left, but I believe it'll still work for the two of you. There are two separate bedrooms joined by a common sitting area. You'll have your own space, even your own bathrooms, and all the doors have locks on them," she said with a wink.

Chris scowled at her, but Charley only hesitated for a second longer and then smiled softly. "That will be just fine, thank you."

Chris didn't let her see his surprise. He thought for sure she'd keep objecting on the grounds that sharing a suite was highly inappropriate for the circumstances. Though really, if they had their own lockable rooms, it wasn't much different than their rooms being separated by a hallway. Still felt more intimate, though, and if the slight pink stain on Charley's cheeks was any indication, she thought so, too. Not much help for it, though, as it was the only room left. They could go where he'd originally planned, but he didn't want to hurt Cass's feelings when they were getting along so well. And maybe Charley would enjoy it so much he could leave her there while he went to check on his properties. Win-win.

Cass had brought a van to transport the rest of the gang, but Chris had a car waiting for him and Charley. They'd be spared being in an enclosed space with his overly attentive friends for at least a little while longer.

Charley glanced back at the van but didn't make any objection when he opened the passenger door of the Hummer he had waiting. In fact, she seemed happy to be climbing into the vehicle with him. Not that he had any illusion it was due to him. She was probably just as happy to get away from his friends as he was. He loved them to death, but they were a lot to handle sometimes, especially when they thought they were on the scent of a brand-new match for him. Being the only single dude in a group of couples was a pain in the ass for a variety of reasons.

Being alone in the car with Charley, however…now that was more appealing. Maybe he could sweet talk her into a good score on her review. Or at least find a nice cliff to chuck her tablet off. Assuming neither of those two plans panned out, he'd at least be able to enjoy a quiet ride with a beautiful woman. Beat the hell out of being trapped with Brooks and the "funny" bunch in the van.

"Ready?" he asked after he'd jumped behind the wheel and started the engine.

"Not even remotely but it's too late to turn back now."

He froze for a second, not sure how to respond to that. A slow grin touched her lips, and she laughed softly. "Yes, I'm ready. Onward!" She gave him a little salute that was so supremely adorable he couldn't help but smile.

Maybe this trip hadn't been such a bad idea after all.

• • •

Had she really just said *onward*? Was it possible to be any more lame?

She resisted the urge to groan and instead fiddled with her phone, bringing up a playlist that always put her in a good mood. If she was lucky, she could listen to her music the whole way to Cass's hotel and be spared any more embarrassing idiocies spewing from her mouth.

"Are we waiting on something?" she asked, wondering why they were sitting there not going anywhere.

"Yeah, we've got to wait for my slow-ass friends and their million bags to get loaded before we can go. We need to follow the van. I have no idea where Cass's hotel is located."

A slight frown furrowed his brow, and while her gut was screaming at her to stay out of it, curiosity got the better of her. "Is it weird going to your ex-girlfriend's hotel? I mean, you guys seem on friendly terms but still…"

He shrugged. "It's a little awkward maybe. Hopefully it's not a bad idea. But seriously, how do you graciously decline a public invite like that? It was big of her to ask and saying no might have given her the wrong idea."

"True. Not much you can do when you get put on the spot like that."

"Exactly. And to be honest, I'm curious about the place. She's been talking about doing something like this forever, but never got up the motivation while we were dating. I'm glad she finally did it. I just hope it's everything she wanted it to be. Sometimes reality doesn't always match the dream."

She almost snorted. "Story of my life."

They finally got underway, and Charley sat quietly beside him, taking in the scenery as they passed. She had put her tablet away, and while she felt almost naked without it, she didn't want to miss all the gorgeous sights they were passing. Besides, if Chris did anything noteworthy, she'd surely remember it and could mark it down later.

She'd caught him trying to take a peek over her shoulder

a few times before she'd put it away, and judging by the confused crinkle around his eyes, she'd been right. He had no clue what all the numbers meant. Hopefully, they added up to him being insured, for both their sakes. Things were going pretty well so far. She hoped.

"Do you come down here often?" she asked, her quiet voice jolting him out of his thoughts.

"A couple times a year. I like to keep an eye on my properties. I usually stay at one of them, so the hotel will be a change."

A million other questions bounced around in her mind, but she didn't voice any of them. She didn't want him to feel like she was interrogating him or anything. Instead, she just looked back out the window, slipping an ear bud into her ear.

"What are you listening to?" he asked, nodding at the phone in her hand.

That telltale warmth heated her cheeks, and she ducked her head, hoping he didn't notice the blush that always plagued her. "My Old School Party playlist."

He raised an eyebrow at that. "Old school, huh? And what's on that?"

"A bunch of eighties' music, mostly."

He full-on grinned at that. "Seriously?"

That seemed to be guys' typical reactions to her obsession with eighties' music. "My mom's a fan. She raised me on this stuff."

He grinned wider.

"What? A lot of it's pretty good!"

"Oh, this I've got to hear."

She tried to dodge him, but he plucked her phone from her hands before she could protest, hit a few buttons on the phone and the Hummer's dash, and in moments Bobby Brown's "My Prerogative" was blaring from the speakers.

"Oh yeah, that's the stuff," he said, shimmying his

shoulders.

She glared at him. "You don't have to make fun of me."

"I'm not. I love this stuff." And then he started belting out the song like it deserved.

She sat riveted to her seat for a second, well and truly stunned. Then she slapped a hand over her mouth to keep from laughing. He was actually giving Mr. Brown a run for his money. There was just no way she'd ever fathomed that not only was Chris a closet karaoke star, but one who knew every lyric to "My Prerogative." She shook her head but couldn't keep her laugh from breaking out. He grinned back at her but kept on singing, adding a few impressive sitting-dance moves while he was at it.

It only took a bar or two before she joined in singing. It was a shame they were following the van and not the other way around, because the show they were putting on was seriously epic.

They were nearing the end of the song when Charley caught movement out of the corner of her eye. Her voice broke off in a strangled gasp.

"What?" Chris asked, throwing a concerned glance her way.

She leaned in her seat as far away from her window as she could get, vaguely aware that she was totally encroaching on Chris's personal space and not giving a flying fart in the wind. Anything to get her farther away from the monster stalking across the glass.

"Oh my God, oh my God, oh my God," she said, her voice growing higher pitched and more frantic with each word.

"What? What is it?" he asked, his head whipping back and forth, trying to see what was going while still keeping them on the dirt road they were bumping down.

The only response she could summon was a terrified screech. She whipped off her seat belt before he could say another word and flung herself out of her seat and half into his.

"What the—"

She yanked off her shoe and began beating at the spider on the window with the ferocity of a...well, of a woman trying to kill the shit out of a huge-ass spider, screaming her head off the whole time. As she was still sitting half in his lap, his control of the car was probably precarious at best. Some part of her terrified brain registered that not only was she exhibiting extremely unsafe vehicular behavior, but she was forcing Chris to do so as well. Not much she could do about any of that, however, because there was a veritable nightmare inching closer to her, even with her shoe flying at it. Maybe because her shoe was flying at it. She was probably just pissing it off, which only freaked her out more.

"Pull over!" she squealed.

"There's no shoulders or anything on this road," he said, though he was laughing so hard he could barely speak. "Hang on. There's a spot ahead that might work."

He gunned it until they reached a section of the road that was wider than the rest, and then stomped on the brakes to stop.

He jumped out, dumping her fully into the driver's seat, though she kept trying to beat the hell out of the mutant spider on the passenger window. Seriously, she'd known they grew bigger down in the jungle, but that thing was unacceptably large. By the time Chris made it to her side and opened the door, all that was left of it was a couple twitching legs sticking out of a pile of goo.

He glanced at her, then back at it, then burst out laughing again. "Think you got it?"

"Can you still tell it's a spider?"

"Yeah."

"Then it's not dead enough."

He laughed, but she wasn't joking. If it was recognizable, it needed more killing. She raised her shoe to whack it again.

"Maybe you better let me have that," he said, plucking it from her hand before she could go all ninja on it again.

"Sorry," she said, smoothing back a few tendrils that escaped from her ponytail with a shaking hand. Her heart still thundered in her chest, and while a nervous laughter was bubbling out of her throat, the very real threat of tears burned hot on its heels. To say she had a phobia of the things was an understatement.

She took a deep breath and tried to calm down before Chris realized how badly she was freaking out. "I really don't like spiders."

"I noticed." He still wore an amused grin, but there was real concern lingering in his eyes. She found that both sweet and mortifying.

"Think there will be any more?"

His eyebrows lifted. "Well, we are in a jungle so..."

She sighed and slumped back into her seat, though she still kept as far from the window as she could. "I was afraid of that."

"No worries. We'll get you a huge flyswatter or something you can carry around."

"Flyswatter? How about a machete."

He laughed. "I'll see what I can find."

He used her shoe to scrape off what was left of the creature, but when he tried to hand the shoe back, she looked at it suspiciously.

"Did you get it all off?"

He frowned slightly, looking it over. "I think so. If not, I don't think what's left can hurt you."

She visibly shuddered. "Yeah, that's not going to work for me."

He grinned again, although the sheepish squint of his

eyes implied he at least felt bad about laughing at her pain. Not that she blamed him. She knew exactly how ridiculous she must look right then. And now that her heart rate was slowing to a more human range again, she could laugh at herself. Hell, if she wasn't able to laugh at her antics, she'd never get through the day.

"Sorry for the freak out," she said.

"Ah, no worries. I've dealt with far worse, believe me."

She shook her head. "Not possible."

"No, seriously. Throw a spider at Brooks and see what happens."

She laughed. "I'll have to do that sometime. Though I doubt he's ever jumped in your lap before."

"Not true. Brooks is…well, Brooks is Brooks. You'll just have to take my word for it that jumping into my lap is one of the tamer things Brooks has done. Though, I will admit, he's never done it in a moving car."

She smiled again, grateful he was being so cool about it and that he was dealing with the aftermath.

He rubbed her shoe in the grass again, making sure nothing remained that might traumatize her. "I promise, it's as clean as I can make it," he said, presenting it over his arm like a waiter in a fancy restaurant presenting a bottle of wine.

"Thanks," she said, though she still looked at it like it might jump from his hands and bite her. The damn thing was covered in spider cooties now. It would have to be burned for sure.

"Allow me," he said. He bent and lifted her foot, slipping the sandal back on. His hand lingered on her leg, and she opened her mouth to comment on it, but her breath caught in her throat and a shiver ran down her spine in spite of the blazing heat.

She should say something. Or pull her leg from his grasp. Or…do something other than sit there slowly strangling on the sensations his lingering fingers created.

He finally seemed to notice he still held her leg, and he hastily let go and stepped back, jamming his hands in his pockets.

Her mouth opened like she was going to say something, but instead she gave him a small smile and a quiet, "Thank you."

He nodded. "Well," he said, clearing his voice and pulling out his phone, "I think we lost the rest of the group. I better call and…"

The van pulled into sight before he could dial, and Brooks and Cole stuck their heads out the window.

"Whatcha doin'?" Brooks asked, his amused gaze taking in Charley half reclined and sideways with her bare leg sticking out of the door and Chris's guilty face.

Chris shot him an irritated look. "Nothing."

"Everything okay out there?" Cole asked, his voice concerned but his face holding as much amusement as Brooks'.

"Yep, fine. Just a minor pest problem," Chris said.

"Ah, come on, man. You aren't that big of a pest," Brooks said.

The laughter from the rest of the van passengers floated out to them, and Charley bit her lip to keep from joining them. Chris closed his eyes and muttered something. Charley wasn't sure, but he might have been counting to ten. Or praying for the strength to not kill his friends.

He ignored the rest of the comments coming from the peanut gallery and looked down at her. "You good?"

"Yes. As long as there aren't any more of those things hanging out in here."

He leaned his large frame into the doorway. "I can't promise that, but if there are, my lap is available whenever you need it."

Her mouth dropped open, but he just grinned and shut her door before hurrying around to the other side.

This trip certainly wasn't panning out the way she expected. Considering she needed to keep everything strictly business, that really wasn't a good thing. And Chris wasn't making it any easier.

In fact, he'd been downright charming all day. Interesting, since he hadn't wanted her along on the trip. So, either he really couldn't help himself—which was possible—or he liked her too much to care—which was improbable. Or, more likely, he thought flirting would butter her up enough to get a good score on his risk assessment and get himself a glowing recommendation.

She sighed and resolved again to keep her head out of Fantasyland and back on the ground where she belonged. She needed to focus on the assessment, get it done and over with, and get back to real life. And hopefully, to a promising new career. Then she could get away from Chris and all the confusion he caused in her head.

Until then, she'd have to keep reminding herself what was at stake. No matter how much her hormones might want to convince her to the contrary, Chris wasn't worth risking her career. Especially when the chances of him being interested in anything more than her professional stamp of approval were slim to none.

She ignored the sharp sting of disappointment that thought caused and stuck her earbuds back in her ears.

She had a life plan, and she was going to stick to it.

Chapter Six

Within the hour, they'd hauled all their luggage to Cass's place and gotten settled into their rooms.

Charley stood in the middle of her gorgeous suite, looking back and forth between the two rooms. They were both beautiful and more luxurious than anything she'd ever stayed in before.

But one was obviously smaller and a bit more generic, containing a nice but normal four-poster double bed with a thin layer of mosquito netting and an upscale but run-of-the-mill bathroom. The other room boasted an incredible hand-carved four poster that would be right at home in a castle somewhere, along with yards and yards of luxurious netting, artfully draped around the king-sized bed that was piled high with the softest-looking pillows she'd ever seen.

And the bathroom…she wandered over to take a peek and stopped short, sucking in a breath. The room was tiled in bright mosaics and sported a massive double-headed walk-in shower and a sunken bathtub that looked more like a small swimming pool. That decided her. Christopher Lachlan was a billionaire. He probably had ten bathrooms like this in his house and got to stay in rooms like this all the time. She didn't. And she wanted that tub.

She went back and got her bags from the common room between the suites and staked her claim in the master room. The guilt and anxiety gnawing at her at the audacity of choosing the better room when Chris would no doubt expect it nearly had her turning back. But another glimpse of that tub kept her where she was. In fact…she glanced down at her phone. She had no idea how long Chris would be gone, but as far as she knew, they didn't need to be anywhere until dinner. She had the time. And she knew just how she'd use it.

By the time the tub was filled with lavender-scented bubbles and steaming water, she had her bags unpacked and was ready to relax. The day had definitely not gone as she'd expected so far. But then nothing about this job had gone as expected. She'd thought she'd spend a day or two shadowing Chris around New York, watching him do whatever it was billionaires did on a workday. And then she'd write up her report, present it to his board and the reps from the insurance company, and be on her way. Hopefully, without any fallout from her slight deception.

Her firm—ex-firm—would be pissed when they found out she'd done the assessment, seeing as how she was no longer working for them. But they wouldn't be able to do anything about it at that point, and both the insurance company and Lachlan Enterprises would be happy enough with her results that they wouldn't question anything. That was the idea, anyway. Though, if she didn't recommend Chris for insurance, things might go south fast. At least on his end.

She tried not to think about that. He wasn't the one she was there to impress. It was the insurance companies she needed to build a relationship with. They were the ones she'd be working with long term, the ones who would mostly be hiring her for assessments. Whether or not Chris was happy wasn't something with which she needed to concern herself.

Easier said than done, especially when she was on an all-expenses paid trip of a lifetime and sleeping half a room away from him.

She pulled an armful of bubbles up to her chin, giving herself a bubble beard like she used to when she was a child. The popping bubbles tickled her nose but did little to dissipate the unease radiating through her at the whole situation. She shouldn't have let herself get talked into this trip. It was so inappropriate on so many levels. Though Izzy had a point about it being a great way to see Chris in his natural habitat, as it were. Still...

Charley scooped up more bubbles and gave herself a hat.

"Oh! Sorry..." Chris's voice sounded from the doorway, and Charley jumped with a squeak. Their eyes met for half a second before he quickly turned around.

"Sorry," he said again. "I didn't realize you were in here..."

"It's fine," she mumbled, pulling as many of the bubbles as she could gather to her chest. Not that he could see anything. She hadn't been stingy with the bubble bath, and she was sunk to her chin in a sea of foam.

"I'll, uh, just wait outside for you," he said, his voice almost shaking with amusement.

"I'll be right out."

"No rush."

No rush? Whatever. Like she could relax now.

He glanced over his shoulder as he pulled the door shut behind him and gave her a sexy little half grin that had her stomach crashing to her toes. "That's a good look on you."

Her jaw dropped, popping the bubble beard she'd forgotten about until that second.

The second the door closed, she climbed out of the tub,

brushing off as many of the bubbles from her body as she could before pulling on the plush robe that hung from the door. She made sure it was wrapped tight about her and hurried into the shared common room where Chris was lounging on the couch while perusing his phone.

The moment she came into sight, he dropped it onto the table and smiled up at her. "Sorry about that. I expected you to be in the other room, and I didn't see your bags when I entered so…" He shrugged, though everything about his demeanor screamed amused rather than contrite.

As for her, her embarrassment evaporated on a wave of irritation at his assumption that she'd automatically leave the best room for him. Despite the fact that she'd been feeling guilty about not doing that herself just minutes before. Still, it was one thing for her to think it, another entirely for him to expect it.

Her annoyance helped her gather her composure, and she was able to tuck her robe under her legs and sit primly and properly on the armchair next to the sofa. If it was one thing she'd learned from a lifetime of doing her utmost to remain in control at all times, it was to fake it until you make it. She'd just act confident and controlled until her equilibrium returned and she was composed in truth.

She gave him what she hoped was a cool and collected smile. "I know the room I chose is slightly better than the other, but I am your guest, after all, and a rather unwilling one at that."

His eyebrow rose. "I've been accused of many things, Ms. Claybourne. Keeping unwilling women as guests has never been one of them. If you wish to return home, you have only to ask."

Her smile warmed a little at that. "Unwilling is probably the wrong word. Reluctant might be better."

He laughed. "That makes two of us. As for the room,

I'm happy for you to stay in whichever one you wish. I *am* theoretically supposed to be trying to impress you, after all."

"Theoretically?" she asked with a slight head tilt. There was no theoretical about it. The man should be kissing her ass every chance he got considering how bad things looked for him at the moment.

"Guess I need to up my game."

She gestured at the grand room behind her. "I think this already borders on over-the-top bribery. Upping your game might be downright criminal."

He chuckled. "One can hope. Sorry again for the whole Peeping Tom routine. I didn't see your bags, so I guess I assumed…"

"I've unpacked them. I despise living out of a suitcase."

He laughed again. "I don't think my bag has been unpacked in over a year. I travel so much I just keep it packed at all times."

"Don't you hate being on the road all the time?"

He shook his head. "I love it. I get a little squirrely if I stay in one place too long. You don't travel much?"

"Not really. I mostly work in the city, and my family is spread out enough we don't get together often. I'm a bit of a homebody, I guess. Give me a cozy blanket, a comfy couch, and a good book or show to binge and I'm happy," she said.

He smiled, though it didn't quite reach his eyes. "Well, to each his own." He stood and grabbed a small duffle from the floor by the couch and headed to the smaller room. "Just a head's up. If you hate going out, you're not going to like tonight's plans much."

"Why is that?" she asked, her stomach doing the familiar anxious flip that had her gripping the side of her chair. "Where are we going?"

But instead of answering, Chris just gave her one of those devastating smiles that had her stomach flipping for all different reasons and disappeared behind his door.

· · ·

Chris watched Charley's face as they neared the entrance to the hotel where the casino was located. He couldn't read her no matter how hard he tried. She seemed…confused maybe? There was a slight furrow to her brow, though she didn't appear to be distressed. Maybe it'd been wrong to talk her into coming with them, but leaving her on her own seemed more wrong.

He'd like to pretend it was because he didn't want her finishing up her evaluation and sending off a damning report when he wasn't paying attention, but that wasn't it. He just didn't like the thought of her sitting all by her lonesome in some foreign hotel while the rest of them were off having fun.

She intrigued him. Everything about her was a walking contradiction. From outward appearances, he'd never think she had a moment's doubt about anything. She seemed like a person who was in control and had her shit together at all times. Impeccable, tasteful clothing. Soft auburn hair falling past her shoulders in tamed, shiny waves that looked like they'd never been out of place. A calm, soothing voice that would probably pacify rabid tigers into lying down for a belly rub. Everything about her painted a picture of a classy, well-traveled, well-educated, worldly woman.

And yet this same woman had fought him over a jug of milk that ended up all over the floor, broken a heel on soft carpeting, nearly crashed his plane, and been caught up to her neck in bubbles and nothing else in a tub he'd assumed was his. For someone so put together, a lot of stuff seemed to go wrong for her. But she dealt with it all remarkably well, he'd give her that.

However, it also made it damn near impossible for him

to figure out what was going on in her head. She was looking around at their surroundings with faint curiosity. He couldn't tell if she was happy to be there, dismayed or scared, or just totally indifferent to it all.

He was leaning toward indifferent when a flash of interest crossed her face and she made a beeline to the roulette table. Costa Rica's gambling halls were definitely different from those in the States. Besides being smaller and generally more subdued, the games differed a bit.

Roulette was one of the more popular games. Well, the Costa Rican version of canasta, which was pretty much the same game only the ball was pulled from a big spinning basket like a good old-fashioned game of bingo. But they did have regular roulette tables, and Charley was already slapping some chips down on numbers and ignoring the scowling dealer who, like most dealers in Costa Rica, seemed to take pride in being rude to everyone. Though that was part of the ambience that made it fun. Once you got used to it.

The ball clunked into the slot for Red 17, and a faint smile touched Charley's lips. Wow. Coming from her, that was quite a reaction. If she'd been in Vegas, or any other person, he'd have expected an excited *woot* or some indication she was thrilled she'd just tripled her bet. But it was Charley they were talking about. And that sort of behavior was frowned on in the Costa Rican casinos, anyway. It was a good thing he'd been sure to warn her and his friends to dress down instead of glamming it up like many did in the States. Well-dressed gamblers were nothing but a huge *Rob Me* sign here. But even in shorts, sandals, and a simple V-neck white T-shirt, Charley still stood out in the crowd. The woman screamed class no matter what she was in.

Even when she was in nothing but a bubble beard and hat floating in a pool of steaming water.

He shook his head to try and get rid of that image,

not that it did him any good. The glorious vision that was Charlotte-Leigh Claybourne in the tub was branded into his brain forever.

And that was a big, big problem. Because the delectable Ms. Claybourne was off-limits. Inaccessible. Forbidden.

And damn if that didn't make him want her more.

But since he really wanted to keep the company he'd busted his ass over for the majority of his adult life, he was going to have to keep his hormones in check and leave good ol' Chuck alone.

Another clunk of the ball and faint grin from Charley signaled another win. And he wasn't the only one who noticed her luck seemed to have changed. A few surly gentlemen across the table from her shot unfriendly looks in her direction, and Chris was by her side before he'd consciously decided to move. She glanced up at him briefly before turning her attention back to the game.

"Do you play?" she asked, laying her chips out on her chosen numbers with the same precision and meticulous care he'd once seen an antiquities dealer handle a 3,000-year-old vase.

"I'm more of a poker man myself," he said, keeping his eyes on the men across the table.

Her eyebrow rose delicately in what he assumed was a question as to why he was vulturing her instead of playing at one of the few poker tables the casino had.

He shrugged and nodded to her growing stack of chips. "You've been here all of ten minutes and seem to be doing rather well. Maybe I'm just hoping to soak up a little luck before I try my hand."

She laughed softly. "Don't soak up too much. I don't generally have much to spread around."

His eyebrow raised at that. "You sure about that? You seem like you're a pro at this."

"Oh, I've been to my fair share of casinos. I'm generally broke before I make it halfway through the doors. It's kind of fun winning for a change."

Before he could say anything to that, someone passing behind her brushed up a little too close, and she jumped with a surprised squeak. As she was leaning over the table to place another bet at the time, her jump set off a truly spectacular chain of reactions that he could only stand there helpless to stop.

Her hand knocked into the woman next to her, which made the woman jerk and dump her drink all over the table and dealer. The dealer, who'd been holding the ball above the spinning wheel, dropped it instead of spinning it around the rim like he should have, and it landed square in Black 32. Half of the gamblers at the table were thrilled. The other half were not. They all made their feelings about the matter very clear. When the dealer tried to retrieve the ball, adamant that it did not count, the gamblers who'd placed "winning" bets on the number set up a ruckus the likes of which had probably never been seen in a Costa Rican casino.

The dealer started shouting at everyone in rapid Spanish, the woman who'd spilled her drink was in tears and fanning at her face like she'd just been accosted by a pack of wild dogs, and the other gamblers were all screaming at the dealer and one another. Until they all, almost in unison, turned toward Charley.

"Oh shit," Chris muttered. He took her arm and started backing her away from the table. "I think we should probably make ourselves scarce," he said, trying to keep his eye on both the group of murderously angry gamblers in front of them, the dealer who was still shouting and gesturing to them, and the trio of armed security guards who were quickly bearing down on them.

"But my chips…" Charley said, pulling against his grip.

"Leave them."

"But…"

"I'll pay you double what you've got there to not fight me on this." Before she could argue again, Chris made an executive decision in the hopes of saving their lives, bent down, and tossed Charley over his shoulder.

She yelped and grabbed at his waist. "What are you doing?"

"Saving our asses, hopefully," he said, throwing some cash at the roulette table both as a peace offering and as a distraction.

"But…"

Chris didn't stick around to see if the cash toss worked or to hear her protests. He just turned on his heel and headed for the door. They passed his group of friends on the way out, every last one of whom was standing and staring with their mouths hanging open. He waved at them in what he hoped they'd understand was a "*we gotta get out of here*" gesture and turned his focus back to the thankfully close front door.

He didn't stop until they were a block away. Even then, he paused only long enough to put Charley down. Then he grabbed her hand and they hauled ass a few more blocks, finally ducking into a smaller hotel that looked mostly reputable. He led Charley into the hotel's bar and collapsed into a chair.

"Well, that was…different," he said, waving the waiter over and pulling out his phone to quickly text his friends their location.

Charley shrugged then ran a hand through her hair and crossed her legs.

He raised an eyebrow at the shrug. "Not a new experience for you?"

"Mr. Lachlan, I have the worst luck in the world. Always have. Idiotic, unbelievable stuff happens to me all the time.

I'm a magnet for misadventure."

The waiter came over and she ordered a bottled water. Chris ordered four shots of tequila.

"You can't leave it at that. Spill," he said.

She shrugged again. "It would take more time than I care to spend on all the insanity that happens in my life. I will say, though, that this is the first time I've been chased out of a Costa Rican casino for dumping a drink on the dealer."

"First for me, too," Chris said with a laugh.

Her lips twitched. "Hang around with me long enough and it won't be your last."

"Is that a threat or a promise?"

"It's a fact."

He threw his head back and laughed like he hadn't done in a long time. "You're not boring, Claybourne. I'll give you that."

She gave in and allowed a full smile to grace her beautiful face. "Glad you think so. It's not the general feeling of most men I've been with, I assure you." Her face blanched. "Not that we're together. I just meant…"

He held up a hand to stave off her sputtering. "I know what you meant."

Their drinks came, and he downed a shot while she sipped at her water. He pushed two of the shot glasses toward her. "You're on vacation for the night. Live a little."

"This isn't a vacation."

"You don't have your little tablet with you."

She tapped her forehead. "Taking mental notes to add later."

He frowned slightly at that. "I want the record to show that the whole being chased from a casino by a mob thing was *not* my fault."

That full, luscious mouth of hers pulled into a soft smile again. "Noted."

She took a deep breath and then sighed and pulled a glass toward her.

His frown deepened. "You don't have to drink if you'd rather not. I certainly don't want this to turn into some afterschool special on peer pressure or anything."

She glanced up at him from under her lashes with an expression he could only call mischievous on her face. "No worries, Lachlan," she said, following his lead with the last name calling. "You're right. I could do with a little vacationing. For a few hours, anyway."

She raised the glass to him in a salute and then downed it. His eyebrows hit his hairline. He'd expected her to sip at the drink, maybe while holding a dainty pinkie up in the air. She surprised him at every turn.

She slammed the drained glass on the table while blowing out a silent whistle. "Ooo, that was good."

His eyes widened as she grabbed a second glass and did the same thing while he just sat and stared at her, his jaw probably scraping the ground like some sort of strangling guppy.

She, on the other hand, was taking in their surroundings with an increasing air of enthusiasm. When her eyes caught sight of the stage at the far end of the bar where the live band had been quietly playing a few sets of generic music, her entire demeanor changed.

"I'll be right back," she said, ignoring his slight grunt of surprise.

By the time Brooks, Leah, Harrison, Nikki, Cole, Kiersten, Izzy, and Cass made it to the bar and dragged some seats up to the table, Charley was strapping on a guitar and testing it out with a few chords.

"What's going on?" Harrison asked, his posh British accent seeming even more out of place than usual.

"No clue," Chris said, his eyes transfixed on Charley, who

was now adjusting the microphone in front of her mouth. She explained to the small audience, in fluent Spanish no less, that the band had kindly agreed to let her sing one of her favorite songs.

"Is she drunk?" Izzy asked.

Chris tore his gaze from the stage long enough to shrug. "Probably. She only had two shots, but she downed them back to back pretty quick, and I have no idea when she's eaten last."

Instead of being dismayed, Izzy grinned. "Two-drink Charley is a friggin blast."

"Can she actually sing and play that thing?" he asked just as the opening notes of the song echoed through the bar. "Never mind," he murmured, his attention riveted to the stranger who had taken over Charley's body on the stage.

His body was already moving in time with the deep notes emanating from her surprisingly talented fingers when she sang the first few words in a sultry voice that had him squirming on his chair. And then the words registered.

He turned to Izzy. "Is she singing The Grinch song?"

Izzy hooted some encouragement at the stage and sat at the edge of her chair, excited energy surging from her. "Oh yeah. She shreds the shit out of this song. She did this for our talent show junior year of high school. We thought for sure she'd be the next Pat Benatar or Pink until…"

Izzy stopped talking, her lips pinched. But before Chris could ask what that was all about, Charley's voice went from sultry to flat-out metal rock goddess, and he was riveted. Her fingers flew over the guitar strings while the drummer and band behind her started picking up on her beat and playing along.

"Holy shit," he said, pretty sure he'd never been so surprised or turned on in his life as he was right in that moment watching his composed, librarian-ish, risk assessor up on that stage giving Axel Rose a run for his money.

"You ain't seen nothing yet," Izzy said.

And she was right.

Charley spent the next four and a half minutes delivering what was hands down the best rock performance he'd ever seen in his life.

It was official. Metal Grinch was his new favorite song. *Ever.*

"Look at him," Brooks said. "He can't take his eyes off her. I double my bet." He pulled out his phone and started scrolling through it.

"Ditto," Cole said.

The rest of the group jumped in with a chorus of double downs and a few who wanted to move their dates up.

The last note of Charley's song faded away, and she stepped back from the microphone, looking a bit dazed. Their eyes locked, only for a moment, but long enough to send an electric shock through him that had him sucking in a breath.

The band members surrounded her, blocking her from Chris's sight. And his friends' conversation finally registered in his brain.

"Wait a second," he said. "You assholes bet on when Charley and I will hook up?"

"Absolutely," Cole said.

"No, we didn't," Kiersten said. Chris relaxed for a second, but he shouldn't have, because her next words had him tensed up again. "The bet is for when you two will get together. You know…like a couple."

He stared at her, mouth slightly open, though he couldn't seem to force any words out. Kiersten had the grace to look a little sheepish, but the guys had no such compulsion.

"Unbelievable," he said.

Brooks snorted. "You can't be that surprised. I'm pretty sure you were part of the pool on every single one of us."

"That's not true," Chris said, though his voice lacked the conviction it needed to get his point across. Mostly because they were right. He scowled at them. "It's not the same."

"Why?" Harrison asked. "Because now you're the one in the hot seat?"

"Yes!" he said, though his irritation only made them laugh harder.

Really, he couldn't get too mad. It's what they did. Placed bets on everything and everyone, *especially* when it came to their love lives.

"We really need to get a new hobby," he muttered.

"Sounds like a plan," Izzy said. "Next time. This time around, I'm in!" She took Brooks' phone from him so she could peruse the pool calendar.

"You're all going to lose. She's off-limits. I touch her and any credibility she has as my risk assessor goes out the window. She's my last shot to get insured. There's no way I'm screwing this up."

That cooled their enthusiasm. For all of three seconds.

"True love will always find a way!" Brooks said and went back to scrolling through the betting pool board with Izzy.

"You're all insane," Chris said.

"Ah, you know we love you," Izzy said, leaning over to kiss his cheek.

"Yeah, yeah," he said, though his attention was only half on them. Charley was still on the stage, speaking to the band members, who seemed very happy with her performance. They weren't the only ones. He could quite happily sit and watch her sing for the rest of his life.

And that was a major problem.

He was so screwed.

Chapter Seven

Charley let the last note die away before she stepped back from the mic and took a deep breath. It had been a very long time since she'd performed anything on stage. She still played when she was home alone. But getting on stage and letting it all go? She hadn't done that since…

The memories rushing back in went a long way toward burning off the pleasant buzz the alcohol had given her. Enough to burn away the residual high of performing in front of a cheering crowd. Performing in front of one person in particular. She looked back into the audience, met his gaze. Those intense eyes that seemed to paralyze her legs and glue her to the spot. That look shook her straight to her core. She hadn't meant to garner his attention by climbing on that stage. She didn't really know what she'd meant to do. She'd pounded those shots, felt the fire flowing through her, seen the stage…and that was it.

She'd forgotten how much performing called to her. It was something she'd said good-bye to long ago. But when she'd seen that stage, seen the guitar, with the adrenaline from the casino fiasco still tearing through her, not to mention all the hormones Chris seemed to have awakened when he'd decided to go all caveman on her...she just couldn't help herself.

Now, it was like Pandora's box had been opened. She needed to cram everything back inside before it took her over and the darkness and panic from the early days after the accident that had nearly claimed her brother's life took over. Again.

She lifted the guitar from around her neck and handed it back to the band member to whom it belonged. He clapped her on the back and offered her a job singing with them any time she wanted. She nodded and mumbled something in response then hurried off the stage and into the hallway, which, thankfully, was where the ladies' room was located. She pushed her way inside and stumbled to the sink.

The cold water she splashed on her face helped. She splashed a few more handfuls on, letting the icy sting snap her out of the whirling misery of her thoughts. Though it was different this time. This time, there was one bright spot in the haze of darkness. Chris, his face shining up at her from the audience. Those beckoning eyes of his offering more than the rest of him was willing to back up, she bet. Didn't matter anyway. He was nothing but the shiny object that would derail her from her plans. The bell to her bird. The squirrel to her dog. Her kryptonite.

Someone handed her a fistful of paper towels, and she jumped then relaxed when she saw Izzy. "Sorry," she said, taking them to pat her face dry. "I didn't hear you come in."

"I noticed. Got a lot going on in that head of yours, don't you?"

Charley met Izzy's gaze in the mirror. "You could say that."

Izzy cocked her head. "Old stuff? Or new stuff?" She said that last bit with a speculative smile Charley didn't like.

"Both. Not that it matters."

"Of course it does."

"Why?"

Izzy sighed and turned around to lean against the sink. "Because you've spent too long letting the old stuff keep you from the new stuff. The accident wasn't your fault. That's why they call it an accident. And Derrick is fine. Continuing to punish yourself for it isn't good for anyone. Especially you."

"Derrick almost died, Iz. He *did* lose an ear. And it *is* my fault. I was the one driving the car."

"It was dark and wet…"

"And I was going too fast."

"You were sixteen."

"Yeah. And I knew better."

"Chuck, you were a kid. Kids make mistakes. You can't control everything all the time. You need to stop beating yourself up about this."

Charley smoothed her shirt down and tucked her hair behind her ears. "That's not what I'm doing."

"Right. That's why you have to be so in control of yourself in every situation that you barely let yourself smile, let alone enjoy life. You're wound so tight you're like a walking time bomb. I don't think you'd be half as klutzy as you are if you'd loosen up a bit."

She might have a point there, but Charley didn't want to admit it. "What you always fail to understand is that I do enjoy my life. I love my job, and I'm going to love being my own boss even more. I like being organized and professional, and I like having my shit together. What's wrong with that?"

"Nothing. Except you don't seem to differentiate between bad risk and good risk. Sometimes you need to leap before you look, you know? And sometimes, you just need to cut loose and have a little fun without worrying about the consequences."

"That's fun for you, Iz. Not me. For me, that sounds like a Class A nightmare. And I'm seriously not having this conversation again," Charley said, throwing the paper towels away.

She headed for the door, but Izzy stopped her. "Fine. I'm sorry. I'll drop it."

"Good. Thank you."

"But…"

Charley tilted her head back and groaned at the ceiling. "You can't help yourself, can you?"

Izzy grinned with her full-on cheeser smile, and Charley laughed. Izzy could always make her laugh.

"I'll drop the part about Derrick. But we still need to have some words about Chris."

Charley frowned. "I don't see why."

Izzy shook her head. "Woman, you are seriously deep in denial if you haven't noticed him noticing you. And you noticing him back."

Charley shifted slightly against the sudden acrobatics in her stomach. She couldn't hide the flush of her cheeks, though. "You're just seeing things you want to see."

"Right. That's why he about chewed through the table watching you up on that stage."

Cue stomach acrobatics on overdrive. "I'm sure you're mistaken."

Izzy snorted. "I'm positive I'm not. I've known Chris a long time now. I've never seen him like this with anyone, not even Cass. He has it bad for you."

"He barely knows me."

"I know. Imagine how much better it would get if he did."

Oh, Charley could imagine it. Seemed like she'd been doing little else but imagining it since the day he tried to steal her chocolate milk.

But she shoved those thoughts back where they belonged

and shook her head. "Even if I believed you, and I don't, it wouldn't matter. He's my client. My first client on my own. If I...if we..." She sighed. "There's no way anything could happen between us. The last thing in the world I want is a reputation for sleeping my way to the top."

"That wouldn't happen."

Charley cocked an eyebrow at her. "That's exactly what would happen. Not to mention, I'd have every male client who ever crossed my door thinking they could do the same thing. After all, I gave it up for one guy on the job. Why not all of them? Not happening. No one would respect me or trust that I knew what I was doing because they'd all assume I'd slept my way to success."

Izzy's jaw clenched, and Charley knew she wanted to argue, but even Izzy wouldn't be able to find a way to refute her logic. It was Working Woman Code 101. It didn't matter how good, smart, successful, or amazing a woman was, the second she slept with someone in the business pool, all her credibility went right out the window. While the man's increased. It was fucked up, but that was life.

"Besides," she continued, "if he *is* interested, it's probably because he wants to get on my good side while I'm evaluating him. He wants me to recommend him, that's all. And if we were to get together, and then I didn't recommend him, he could come back and say it was because of what happened or all kinds of other stuff. There are a million ways this could bite me in the ass. It would be nothing but a massive HR nightmare."

"Chris would never do that. If he's interested in you, it's because he really likes you. Not any other reason."

"According to you. But how would I ever really know? And how would he ever really know I wasn't just with him to get ahead? There's no way an actual relationship would work between us. And I'm not interested in some vacation fling that would do nothing but tank my career before it even got started."

Izzy pouted for a second but eventually nodded her head. "Okay. I guess you make a few good points."

"Thank you."

"I still say you guys are perfect for each other, though."

Charley shrugged. "Doesn't make much difference now."

Izzy got that gleam in her eyes that usually meant she was up to something. "We'll see."

She turned on her heel and headed out the door.

"Izzy."

She kept walking, so Charley hurried after her. "Izzy, what do you mean, we'll see?"

This didn't bode well.

• • •

Chris opened the door to the suite he shared with Charley and looked around as he stepped inside. Charley and Izzy had disappeared after she'd left the stage, which had probably been a good thing. He'd definitely been ready to say and do a few things he would have regretted later. Still was, if he was being honest, but he had a little better handle on himself.

At least he'd thought so, until he saw her sitting at the small table by the window in the soft glow of her tablet, glasses he hadn't known she'd worn perched on her nose. What was it about a pair of glasses that could make a woman look so damn sexy? He had a sudden vision of her jumping onto the table, ripping the glasses off, shaking her hair out, and breaking into a head-banging rendition of "Welcome to the Jungle" or some other song she could rock her ass off to.

He shook his head, trying to clear that mental picture. Unfortunately, it would probably be years before he got her out of his head. If ever.

She'd turned her tablet into a mini laptop with a mobile keyboard and was busily typing away. Probably destroying his career with each click of the keys. In hindsight, taking a risk assessor out to a South American casino might have been a bad idea. Considering how they'd had to exit the place, he couldn't imagine *that* report going well. He doubted she'd enjoyed the feel of her soft body bouncing on his shoulder as much as he did.

Or maybe she had…she hadn't struggled or protested aside from her initial surprise. He'd have to ponder more on that later. Getting her drunk afterwards probably hadn't helped his cause, either. Though she *had* seemed to enjoy herself. Right up until she ran out.

She glanced up when the door closed and nodded at him with one of her soft, careful smiles that betrayed nothing of what she was really feeling.

"You disappeared on us. Glad to see you made it back okay," he said, coming over to lean on the back of the other chair at the table.

She frowned slightly. "Izzy said she texted everyone when we left so you would know where we'd gone. Did she not do so?"

"She did."

Her brows lifted a fraction in question, but he didn't really have an answer for why he was acting like a jilted date. She certainly didn't owe him any apologies or explanations. And there wasn't much he could say that would make any sense, so he decided to take the safe road and change the subject.

"Tomorrow I'll be inspecting a few properties in the morning, and in the afternoon, I'll probably go hiking or something. You're welcome to hang out here if you'd prefer. I can't imagine you'll have much fun following me around all day."

She closed the tablet down and took off her glasses. "I

thought following you around all day was the reason I was here."

"True. Guess I was trying to give you an out if you wanted one. Seeing as how our first outing went so well."

Her lips twitched at that. "Yes, well, that wasn't entirely your fault."

"Really?" He crossed his arms. "I would have said that none of it was my fault."

She shrugged. "I suppose it depends to which part of the evening we are referring. Though I'm happy enough to accept partial responsibility and leave it at that."

He laughed. "Well, we shouldn't run into any angry mobs tomorrow, so you should be safe."

That half smile peeked out again. "Thank heavens for that."

"Shouldn't run into any other bands desperately looking for rocking lead singers, either."

Her eyes narrowed, and her cheeks flushed a faint pink that made him want to smooth his fingers over her skin to see if it was as warm as it looked.

"Thank heavens for that, too," she said.

"Oh, come on. You can't shred up a stage like that and then just pretend it never happened." He dropped onto the couch. "Spill it. How does someone…" He looked her over, waving his hand in her direction.

"Someone like me?" she asked.

"Someone in your line of work," he said, not liking the way she'd said *someone like me*, as if she wasn't completely perfect, but rather defective or deficient in some way. "Come on. What's the story there?"

She sat on the arm of the couch, as far away from him as she could get without being obvious about it. Even though it was totally obvious.

"There's not much to tell. I was in a band with some

friends when I was younger. And then I gave it up. End of story."

"Uh, that's not a story. That's barely a highlight reel. I mean, seriously, how does a woman go from rock goddess to risk assessor? You looked like you were having the time of your life on that stage tonight. Like it was something you really loved."

"It's called performing."

He cocked an eyebrow at her. She sighed and looked down at her feet for a second and then shrugged. "Something happened that made me realize there were more important things in life. And no, I don't want to go into more detail than that."

"All right, fair enough," he said, wanting to push her on whatever it was that put that sad look in her eyes, but he had no business interrogating her. And the last thing he wanted to do was make her sad, which was what his current line of questioning seemed to be doing.

"Well," he said, getting to his feet. "I want to get an early start tomorrow so I can get those properties inspected and have a little fun before it's time to leave tomorrow night."

"Where are we off to next?"

"Spain."

Her eyes widened. "What, are we going to go run with the bulls or something?"

Chris just smiled and headed to his room. Why spoil the surprise?

"We aren't going to do that, are we?"

He kept walking, his smile growing wider.

"Mr. Lachlan? *Chris*?"

He waited until the door was closed before he let loose the laugh he'd been holding back. The woman was a pain in his ass, but she was a lot of fun to rile up.

Chapter Eight

Charley had spent the day with Chris at three different properties, each a stunning oasis that she'd have gladly sacrificed a week or two of her time to carefully inspect.

And she had to admit, Chris didn't do anything in those few hours that raised any red flags. In fact, he was the model businessman. Professional and focused, if a bit more laid-back than your average billionaire entrepreneur. Then again, it wasn't his business practices that were in question—it was what he did when he wasn't working.

She could see his point about needing to inspect the properties in person. If he had a really good manager he could trust completely, it might not be as necessary. But employees like that were hard to find. And even if there were someone in place that he could count on, being able to check on things himself both gave him peace of mind that everything was running smoothly and kept his employees on their toes. Even she could see that things might grow a little lax if it was known the boss was never going to show up.

So, that worked in his favor. While there was some risk

in traveling all the time, there was certainly good reason for doing so, and he did seem to take all normal precautions when on the road, for which she was happy to give him credit. She didn't know how much of a difference it would make since there was still the matter of his extreme sports-loving past times to address. But for the business traveling side—points for him!

And then there was the play side. What he did after work. Things that were rapidly tanking his chances for insurance approval. Things like climbing on an ATV to go tearing up the jungle. Things he wanted to share with her so she could see how safe they were.

She sighed and finished tying the bandanna around her face and then grabbed the helmet, making sure it fit snuggly around her head before strapping it on.

"Why can't we just go on a regular hike?" she asked.

"Oh, come on," he said. "You can't really object to these." He gestured at the ATVs they were sitting on. "They're perfectly safe. They have four, big, sturdy wheels, you're wearing more pads than a linebacker, and you even get to control how fast they go. What can you possibly object to?"

"Really?" she asked. "You underestimate my objecting abilities if you think I can't find anything. Do you have any idea the safety hazard these things present? Seriously, if I showed you the stats, you'd be much less enthusiastic to get on them."

She cocked her head at him, looking him up and down, from his animated grin to the way his body nearly vibrated with excitement. She rolled her eyes.

"Never mind. Somehow, I don't think safety ratings matter too much to you."

He laughed. "They are perfectly safe. Plus, these are the best way to get around out here. They can get places cars can't go, travel some rougher terrain, really get us up in the jungle where all the cool stuff is."

"We do have legs, you know. I think they'd get us up there just as well."

He laughed again. "Not up where I'm taking you. And trust me, before you say that maybe you don't want to go somewhere you need to ride these to go—you'll *want* to go. What you're going to see once we reach the top is an absolute to-die-for sight. Once in a lifetime."

She sighed and leaned forward to grip her handlebars tighter. The butterflies in her stomach had turned into hummingbirds, but even she had to admit it was at least partially from excitement. She'd always wanted to ride these things as a kid. Before the accident. And flashes from that accident were harder to ignore when the vehicle she was on didn't have seat belts. Or doors. Or a roof.

Chris wrapped a bandana with a grinning skull mouth on it around his face and let out a loud, "Wooo!"

She shook her head, though she couldn't help but smile. Really, how could two people be more different? Yeah, he was fun to look at, and he'd be a lot more fun to do a few things with. A *lot* of fun. And she even had to admit she was starting to like being with him. He was fun. He made her laugh and definitely kept her on her toes. Being with him would never be boring.

Then again, being with him would probably require a lifetime supply of Xanax. Or a really good internet connection, because the only way she would ever get to see him would be via email and video chat. Because while she stayed at home building the business she'd always wanted, he'd be off trying to break his neck in multiple countries around the world.

Not that any of that mattered anyway. She was there to do a job, and so was he. Any other ridiculous fantasies her brain tried to cook up were nothing but that. Fantasies.

"Are you ready?" he asked.

"As much as I'll ever be."

"Okay then," he said, strapping on his helmet. "Let's go!"

He nodded to the guide that they were ready and revved up the engine on his ATV. Charley took a deep breath and released the brake on her own machine. It lurched forward. Chris looked over his shoulder, waiting for her.

"Just ease up on it," he said.

She released a long breath and slowly eased off the brake, giving it a little gas at the same time. This time, the take-off was much smoother. Chris gave her a huge grin and gave his own some gas, doing a little pop-a-wheelie while he shouted, "Woohoo!"

She rolled her eyes. "Show off."

It took her a few minutes, but she finally got the hang of giving the deathtrap underneath her just enough gas so she wasn't moving at a crawl without going so fast she thought she'd die. After a few more minutes, she actually found herself having fun. The ATVs really did allow them to travel places a car could never go. They threaded through the thick trees down a dirt path for quite a while before emerging on the banks of a creek. She hesitated a moment, but Chris zipped up the creek bed without so much as pausing, so she threw caution to the wind and followed.

She mostly stayed out of the water, but Chris darted in and out of the shallow creek, his infectious laughter ringing out as he sent sprays in all directions. Far from disapproving or being overly cautious as she usually would be, she found herself laughing along with him. Despite her best efforts, it wasn't possible to stay indifferent to him. He was like a great big ball of golden sunshine that warmed and cheered everyone around him, no matter what their intentions. The man was contagious.

He mostly traveled ahead of her as he liked to go quite a bit faster than she preferred. But every few minutes, he'd wait up so he could ride along with her, pointing out exotic wildlife and beautiful plants and flowers. While she never would have thought to use this mode of transportation on her own, she could definitely see the merits.

And while it might be a little riskier than a car, she had to admit that they took every precaution to be as safe as possible. The ATVs seemed very well maintained, they were definitely stable and sturdy, she was padded and helmeted, and they had a seemingly knowledgeable guide there to keep them on the right path. She hated to admit it, but Izzy had been right.

Charley had seen similar pictures of Chris on these contraptions on his Instagram account. And initially, she'd counted his preference for them as a negative. However, with all the precautions she could see that he took, and now that she'd experienced them for herself, she could see she'd been wrong with her initial assessment, something she would've never discovered had she not come on this trip.

She watched him as he splashed through the water, spraying the guide. Watched as he threw his head back to laugh, every rock-hard, solid ounce of him radiating life and happiness and vitality. And the small ball of fear that had taken up permanent residence in her brain after that accident began to unravel. There was no room for it when she was in his presence.

She hated that her entire job was to try to curtail any of that exuberance in him. Because in all honesty, what would make the insurance company very happy and much more comfortable insuring him was if he agreed to give up any sort of extreme sport and spend his days chained to his desk and his nice safe office. But a life like that would probably kill the man. She could no more see him in a suit and tie gazing out his high-rise window day after day than she could see herself hopping from country to country spending her days going from one adrenaline rush to the next. She'd had more fun on this trip so far than she had thought possible. But it was one thing to have an adventure, quite another to live your entire life that way.

She still craved some stability.

"Come on, slowpoke!" he called back over his shoulder. "We're almost there!"

She grinned and gave her ATV a little more gas, gasping with the thrill that rushed through her as she shot forward, zooming after him.

Then again, there was a lot to be said for living your life to the fullest. Maybe she should take a page or two from his book. Or at least a paragraph.

· · ·

Chris smiled as she caught up to him. She might try to pretend like she didn't have an adventurous bone in her body, but her smile said otherwise. He couldn't wait to see the look on her face when they got to their final destination. He could guarantee she'd never seen anything like it.

They traveled for another half an hour, weaving in and out of the jungle as they climbed up the mountain. Finally, they got to where he had been taking her. He knew the exact moment she caught sight of the waterfall. He could hear her gasp even over the roar of their engines.

She slowed her ATV, bringing it to a stop, and he pulled up beside her.

"Oh, wow," she said, staring at the magnificent sight ahead of them.

He smiled and nodded, completely understanding her reaction. The falls weren't the largest in the country by any means. But they were breathtakingly beautiful. The water fell from about twenty feet above them down a vegetation-covered cliff into a crystal clear pool below. The clearing looked as though a giant had scooped out a chunk of the jungle, leaving a clear, lush oasis in the middle of the thick trees. The sun glinted off the water that beckoned invitingly.

"Come on," he said, jerking his head toward the waterfall. "Let's get a closer look."

She gave him a smile that would warm the dark corners of his heart for the rest of his days and took off, just as eager as he was to get to the falls. When they got there, they parked their ATVs, and she climbed off, pulling off her helmet.

"Can we swim?" she asked. He raised his eyebrows, surprised that she would ask before he made the suggestion. He must be rubbing off on her.

"Absolutely. Race you to the water." He took off running, and she followed behind him, laughing.

They wasted no time in stripping off their outer clothing. He had instructed her to wear a swimming suit, and he'd been trying to guess at what she would wear all day. Of course, his mind conjured up several tantalizing images of tiny string bikinis or, better yet, nothing at all. But he suspected she leaned more toward a nice pair of shorts and baggy T-shirt.

Okay, maybe not that extreme. But at the very least a fully covered one piece.

He was pleasantly surprised at her sporty black boy shorts and dark teal halter top ensemble. Tasteful, comfortable, sporty even, while still leaving enough skin bare to actually enjoy the water.

"You first," she said, nodding at the rippling pool. He laughed.

"I was always taught that it was ladies first," he said.

She shook her head. "Please, be my guest."

He shrugged and then took a running leap into the water, executing an impressive cannonball, if he did say so himself. He emerged and ran a hand over his face and up through his hair, flicking off the water droplets. She stood like a little statue on the banks, her eyes glued to his bare, wet chest.

Hmm, so she wasn't as unaffected by him as she liked to pretend.

He ran a hand down his chest, following the lines down the planes of his stomach, brushing away the water. Not because the beaded drops bothered him. But because even from where he stood, he could see her chest hitching with her uneven breaths and her nipples beading through her suit. Oh yes. She was liking the show as much as he was enjoying putting it on for her. He wondered if she'd had any fantasies about what he would be wearing while they swam. And if those fantasies involved stripping off whatever it was.

He closed his eyes, trying to force that image out of his head. He had no business fantasizing about her at all. He didn't need a risk assessor to tell him what a bad idea it would be for them to get involved. Never mind the fact that doing so could put everything he was trying to save at risk. But even if she believed he wanted her for her and not just so he could get on her good side for a good review, their different lifestyles would never mesh well. He'd either be begging her to go with him on his adventures or trying to get out the door without her wrapping him in bubble wrap. If she let him go at all.

That thought brought him up short. What the hell was he thinking? Meshing lifestyles? He hadn't thought about being in any sort of relationship with anyone since Cass. He barely knew Charley. Why on earth would he be thinking about her in terms of anything other than maybe a vacation fling? He certainly wasn't relationship material and had no intention of ever being in one again. And frankly, with all her hang ups, she didn't seem like great relationship material, either. Then again, she was definitely *not* a one-night stand.

He shook his head and dove back under the water, letting the shock of the cold water slap some sense into him. Charley was off-limits. Period. So, fantasies of any kind were off the table.

He swam to the middle of the pool and waited for Charley to finish getting in. She entered the water much more slowly than he had, taking her time to carefully pick her way across the pool bed. When she was about hip deep, she surged forward, immersing the rest of her body to her neck. The look of utter bliss on her face sent several more fantasies cascading through his mind of other ways he could conjure that look.

She waded over to where he stood, though the water that only came to his chest lapped at her shoulders.

"Was it worth the ride on the deathtraps?"

She laughed, wiping her hands across her face. "More than worth it."

"So you're not going to count any of this against me?"

He'd said it with a smile, but she frowned. "I'm not out to get you, you know. I'm just—"

"I know," he said, holding up a hand. "I didn't mean to imply anything. Just...a bad joke."

He winked, and she gave him a hesitant smile. "There's nothing to count," she said. "As far as I can tell, you took every precaution and were safe as possible. When approached responsibly, I can see how an excursion such as this is just as safe as any other."

He nodded, pursing his lips. "Well, well. Never thought I'd see the day that you would admit something like that."

She rolled her eyes. "I'm not some crazy uptight monster. But..." She sucked in a deep breath and slowly let it out again, shaking her head with a faint smile. "When you assess risk for living, it's a little difficult to not see the dangers in every situation you're in."

Her eyes quickly flicked over him, and her cheeks flushed. Somehow, he didn't think she was referring to his job anymore.

"I can see that," he said, catching and holding her gaze. He took a step closer, giving her a slow smile as the red in her cheeks deepened. "As long as you don't let the fear of those risks rule your life."

She stared at him a few seconds longer and then turned her head to gaze back up at the waterfall. "I'm working on that," she mumbled.

He reached out to touch her arm but stopped just short of making contact. What was he doing? This was the one woman on the planet he could not make a move on. At least until the whole assessment thing was over. And yet, he couldn't seem to stop himself.

"Charley."

She looked back at him, but before he could get anything else out, her eyes widened and her mouth dropped open. Oh, no. He knew that look. He managed to brace himself half a heartbeat before she launched herself at him and climbed him like a howler monkey climbing a tree.

"Something touched my leg," she said in between panicked shrieks.

He tried to look through the water at what might have scared her, but that was easier said than done when he had his arms full of terrified female.

She wrapped her legs around his waist and her arms around his neck. But he didn't have time to enjoy that because she immediately tried to climb higher, flinging a leg over his shoulder while she tried to maneuver to his back and keep as much of her body out of the water as possible.

He, on the other hand, was struggling to remain upright while scouring the water and laughing his ass off.

"Charley," he said, gasping between laughs. "I don't think there's anything in here that can hurt you."

She was now on his back, one leg still draped on his shoulder while she clung on to his head for dear life and tried to get her other leg around his other shoulder to get her entire body out of the water like some demented game of chicken fight.

"Charley!" He gripped her thighs, laughing so hard he wasn't sure he could keep holding her. "There's nothing there. I promise."

"Something touched me," she said, peering into the water from her vantage point. "It felt like a snake or something."

"It was probably just a fish. And I guarantee, no matter what it was, you've scared it away."

Her grip on his head loosened enough that he was able to look up at her. "I promise, there is nothing in this water that will eat you."

Except maybe him. But only if she invited him to, and since that wasn't going to happen, she was as safe as she could get in a South American jungle.

She didn't look like she believed him, but she took a long, shuddering breath and slid down. A move that stole his own breath.

He supported her as best he could as she slid down his back, keeping his arms behind him and wrapped around her, savoring every second of skin-on-skin contact. Her feet touched the bottom, but she didn't let go of him. He turned so he was facing her, his eyebrows raised.

"Thanks for not tossing me off," she said with a sheepish smile.

He chuckled. "You had a vice grip on my head. I don't think I could have if I wanted to."

"Yeah, sorry about that," she mumbled, her cheeks flaming bright red again. But she still hadn't let go of him, keeping an arm around his waist.

"Ready to get out?"

"Yeah," she said, but she made no effort to move, frowning at the bank.

He laughed again. "No worries. I got ya."

He scooped her up in his arms. She let out a strangled gasp but didn't object. She just wrapped her arms about his neck and held on tight while he carried her out of the water. Once they were out, he took his time setting her down on her feet. And again, she made no protest. A shiver ran through her body, and she opened her mouth like she was going to say something but then changed her mind. He ran his hands up her arms, mentally screaming at himself to let her go. Nothing good could come of continuing whatever was happening between them.

He gave her shoulders a light squeeze and stepped back, despite every cell in his body screaming in protest.

"We better get back. It'll be dark soon."

Panic quickly replaced whatever emotion had been clouding her eyes, and she nodded, turning on her heel and marching to the ATVs before he could say another word. He laughed quietly and shook his head.

One thing was for sure—he wasn't the only one feeling whatever this was between them. He also wasn't the only one worried about it, if that little frown that had creased her brow was any indication. Acting on it would be a very bad idea. Well...it would be fucking fantastic, but the consequences not so great. He could lose his position if her assessment was determined to be suspect. Her firm would certainly not be happy if she slept with a client.

But whatever this was between them was growing stronger and harder to ignore.

The question was... What were they going to do about it?

Chapter Nine

Charley woke her second morning in Spain and lay still, taking a moment to soak in her luxurious surroundings.

They'd been at the Westin Palace in Madrid for two days now, in the Royal Suite. It was far and away the most beautiful place she'd ever stayed. And not just because of the gorgeous accommodations.

She'd never in her wildest dreams thought she'd be in Spain. She could hardly believe she was there. Until she'd met Chris, she had never even left the country. And here she was a world traveler, already in her second country and, knowing Chris, who knew how many more before she would return home?

She'd expected this trip to be tedious, at best. She didn't even want to think about her worst-case scenario. Though it had something to do with being locked in a cage surrounded by sharks or spelunking through spider-infested caves. So far, though, the trip had been…well, pretty fantastic. Aside from the whole getting chased out of the casino thing and momentary flashes of terror that Chris's little excursions sparked, she'd enjoyed herself much more than she thought possible. Of course, today was a new day. Who knew what he had in store for them now?

And speaking of Chris and sparks…she closed her eyes again and let out a long, shaky breath as every second of their interlude under the waterfall replayed in her mind.

She'd been legitimately terrified when whatever that slimy creature had been brushed by her leg. And when she'd climbed up Chris's tall, strong body, the only thing she'd been thinking was that she wanted to escape the certain death that was swimming around in the water.

But once she was safely perched on top of him, a whole lot of other issues had made themselves glaringly obvious. One, her body had been very, very happy to be wrapped around him. Two, her brain stopped telling her to get out of the danger zone and started coming up with all kinds of really fun ways to take advantage of the position she'd managed to put them in. And three, as far as she could tell, he would have been totally on board with all of it.

And all of the above added up to be a serious problem.

Before she could stress over it more, her phone buzzed, and she grabbed it with her heart in her throat. The rush of disappointment that flashed through her when she saw it wasn't him was further sign that she was teetering on a dangerous precipice.

She put the phone on speaker and flopped back on her pillows. "Hey, Izzy. What's up?"

"You sound like you're in a lovely mood. How's the trip going?"

Charley sighed. "Okay."

Izzy laughed. "Yeah, sounds like it."

"Sorry, I just woke up. Everything really is fine."

"You guys jetted out of here so fast the other day, I didn't get a chance to say good-bye."

"Yeah, sorry about that. Chris seems like he flies by the seat of his pants most of the time."

Izzy snorted. "Understatement of the year." She paused. "So…how are things?"

Charley frowned. "Fine. Actually, it was probably a good idea to come on this trip. I have rethought a few of my previous assessments."

"Just a few, huh?"

"I think he still takes some unnecessary risks. But I've also been able to see the precautions he takes."

"See! I told you."

"Yeah, yeah."

"So, are you going to recommend him then?"

Charley sighed and rolled to her side, tucking a pillow beneath her cheek. "I still don't know."

"Um-hmm. Well, are you going to sleep with him then?"

"Izzy!" Charley sat up and grabbed the phone. "What kind of question is that?"

"Uh, the good kind? Come on, you two would be amazing together. And he totally likes you."

Charley pulled the pillow to her lap so she could bury her face in it and groan. "Does he? Or is he just being nice to me so I'll score him better?"

"He wouldn't do that."

"Maybe. Even if he wouldn't, that's what everyone would think if they found out. That I was stupid enough to get played. Or slutty enough I'll go around sleeping with clients. Not quite the business rep I was hoping to build with this job."

"Are you seriously slut shaming yourself?"

Charley sighed again. "No. Just being realistic about what would happen if I gave in to this…this…whatever it is and people found out. I'd be done."

"You're in Spain. Who's going to find out?"

"Seriously? Even the toddler across the hall has a cell phone. *Someone* would find out."

Izzy was quiet for a few seconds before answering. "I guess. It's a shame, though."

"Yeah, it is."

"Ha! I knew it! You *do* like him!"

Charley laughed and sat up. "Okay, this is getting way too junior high for me. I've got to go."

"All right, well, call me later. And Charley…"

"Yeah?"

"Please do everything I would do."

Izzy hung up mid-laugh, and Charley shook her head. "That girl is nuts."

She got up and threw on a pair of comfy linen pants and a soft white shirt and went to the window to look out on the square in front of their hotel. Their suite overlooked the Fuente de Neptuno—the Fountain of Neptune. A gorgeous work of art that she could, and had, stared at for hours.

The day before, Chris had had a conference call with his board, something that had lasted far too long and put him in a less than stellar mood. While he'd remained professional and courteous with her when she'd met him for dinner that evening, there was definitely a spark missing from his normal overwhelming vitality. He'd shocked her by excusing himself and going to bed early.

She'd spent the evening soaking in the gorgeous bath in the black and gold marble bathroom in her half of the suite, after which she'd curled up with a book in the suite's library. While she hoped Chris would be back to his perky self, she had to admit, it hadn't been a bad way to spend an evening. Especially after the whirlwind she'd already been on.

A knock sounded at her door, and she told Chris—who else would it be—to enter.

He pushed open the door, and she braced herself for

the now-familiar rush of tingling excitement that always accompanied his appearance. The little half grin he gave her sent that rush into overdrive, and she couldn't help but smile back.

"Good morning," he said. "Ready?"

She cocked an eyebrow. "For what?"

"I've got a few things planned."

Her stomach dropped at that. With Chris, that could mean anything.

He barked out a laugh. "What do you think I've got planned that would put that expression on your face?"

"I don't know. Base jumping from the top of the hotel? Bungee jumping from a helicopter? Fencing with real swords while rollerblading around the fountain?"

"All of those are spectacular ideas."

She inwardly groaned. The last thing she wanted to do was put any ideas in his head.

He laughed again. "Stop looking so worried. I just thought we'd do a little sightseeing."

"Oh," she said, giving him a relieved smile. "I think I can handle that."

"Good. Shall we?" He held out his hand and waited patiently for her to take it.

She shouldn't. It was too familiar. And she wanted to too badly. She was also overthinking this in the extreme, but every little move she made seemed to mean something more when it came to him.

He lifted an eyebrow, his lips twitching with amusement. She rolled her eyes and put her hand in his.

As a punishment—or reward—for her hesitation, he kept holding her hand and didn't show any sign of letting go, even after they'd reached the lobby.

• • •

Chris knew he should let go of her hand, but he really didn't want to. Her fingers curled around his felt good. Right. And he had precious little of that in his life right now. Since she showed no sign of it bothering her, he kept holding on to her as he led her through the lobby.

Lucas joined them at the door, and they headed out into the bright sun.

Charley raised a surprised eyebrow at the sight of Lucas. He hadn't been along with them on their excursions in Costa Rica. But she didn't say anything.

"My board feels I should be better protected when walking about a major city," he said, nodding at Lucas, who just smiled at Chris's petulant tone. "With you along for the ride, they don't want me taking any unnecessary risks."

"Ah," she said. "Well, they have a point. You *are* an important person. Your safety is of the utmost importance. And Lucas is your head of security, so you might as well let him do his job."

"Thank you, miss," Lucas said.

Chris scowled. "Don't encourage him."

Charley laughed, and Chris shook his head. "Come on. I want to show you the whole city, and we only have a few hours."

He wasn't kidding. He wanted to show her everything. The way her face lit up when they came across something she found particularly interesting or beautiful was intoxicating. He loved exploring the city, but seeing everything anew, through her eyes, was an experience in and of itself.

He'd slowly come to realize that Charley was as captivated by the world as he was. She just came at it differently. Where he was full balls to the wall, grab life by its horns, go down screaming, she snuck up on it. Studied it. Savored it. Like someone indulging in a rare and especially delicious treat. She might go about it with a little more poise and control, but she loved every second of what the world had to offer.

Maybe they weren't so different after all.

They spent the morning exploring all the sites within walking distance of their hotel, and when their legs were about to fall off from overuse, Chris brought her to a tiny, hole-in-the-wall restaurant that he always frequented when in the city. Tucked away in a cobblestoned alleyway, it wasn't a place tourists often frequented, which made it ideal for him. And the food was to die for.

They took their time eating, but he couldn't wait to show her the surprise he had in store. He'd had to pull a few strings—okay, a lot of strings—but it would be worth it to see her face.

He'd had Lucas arrange for a car while they ate, and by the time he paid their bill, their transportation was waiting.

The Royal Palace lay a short distance from their hotel and was open to tourists. While the Spanish royal family didn't actually live there, reserving it instead for state occasions, it was still considered the official royal residence. And for someone who loved art, culture, beauty, and history, it was definitely a sight Charley couldn't miss.

It was well worth the favors he'd called in to see her eyes light up when they walked inside. They followed along on the regular tours, but once those were over, Chris took her to one of the restricted sections where a private tour guide waited for them.

"What are we doing?" she asked.

"I pulled a few strings," he said. "This lovely lady is going to take us on a tour of the sections of the palace that most people don't get to see."

"Are you serious? What kind of strings did you have to pull to make this happen?"

He shrugged. "The king owed me a favor."

She stopped short, her eyes wide. "The king? As in the

King of Spain?"

"Yeah." And then he flashed her a big grin, grabbed her hand, and pulled her along behind him as the tour guide led them from one opulent room to another.

Once their tour was over, he led her outside to where Lucas waited with the car.

"Are we going back to the hotel?" she asked.

"I thought we could use a little dinner first."

"Oh? Another hidden gem of a restaurant? That last one was fantastic."

"Actually, I thought it might be fun to have a little picnic. Enjoy this weather that we're having. It's not too far away, but I thought you might prefer a ride."

She slid into the car with a grateful sigh. "I thought I was in much better shape than this. But apparently walking from dawn until dusk takes more of a toll than I thought."

He laughed. "Sightseeing with Chris Lachlan isn't for the faint of heart."

Lucas drove them to the Temple of Debod, an ancient Egyptian temple that had been gifted to the city of Madrid in the sixties. Charley sat forward with a gasp, almost pressing her face against the window. The temple was a gorgeous sight in the daylight, set in a beautiful park in the middle of a reflecting pool. But at night, with the stone walls and arches lit from within and people lounging on the surrounding lawns, it was truly spectacular.

"This is where we're having dinner?" she asked.

"Does it meet with your expectations?"

She sat back and gave him a look he couldn't quite interpret. "Everything you've done this entire trip has exceeded my expectations."

"That could be taken as good or bad," he said with a chuckle.

She smiled and squeezed his hand, looking back out the

window.

"This is good. Very, very good."

He gathered up the picnic supplies, and they chose a spot a little apart from the rest of the people. Lucas stood a discreet distance away, keeping an eye on them while they dined on a scrumptious feast that the hotel had put together for them. When their stomachs were full, Charley flopped back on the blanket and released a deep sigh.

"If this is how all your business trips are, then I can understand why you prefer to spend most of your time traveling."

He laid back next to her, propping his head on his arms. "Yeah, you can't really beat this, can you?"

"And you didn't even risk your neck once today. That might be a record."

"Oh, ha ha. I'm not that bad."

She looked over at him, eyebrows raised.

He laughed again. "I guess it's all a matter of interpretation."

Somewhere nearby, someone began playing a Spanish tune on the guitar. A rousing round of cheers echoed from the people around them, who began getting to their feet and dancing in the moonlight. Chris glanced over at her. He probably shouldn't ask her to dance. It wasn't exactly the most professional thing to do. Then again, nothing about that day had felt professional. He'd enjoyed every second with her. In fact, it felt more like a tenth date than escorting a business colleague around a foreign city.

Screw it.

He stood up. They'd had an incredible day. They were full of good food and beer some local vendors were sort of illegally selling. The night was beautiful, and there was music and dancing. There was no way he was passing up this opportunity.

He held out his hand to her, and this time she didn't hesitate before she took it. He pulled her to her feet and into his arms and spun her around. She laughed and held on, and they settled into a rhythm, holding each other in the moonlight on the banks of the ancient temple. Everyone else seemed to disappear. The city itself melted into oblivion.

He didn't know what was going on between them or what would happen in the future. He knew in the light of day that this would be a bad idea. But at that exact moment in time, he didn't care.

He held her in his arms, and nothing had ever felt so right. So, for that one moment, even if it was doomed to end the moment the sun rose, he was going to take what he could and be grateful for it.

He'd worry about the consequences later.

Chapter Ten

How she ended up dressed all in white with a red bandana around her neck waiting on a herd of massive horned animals to charge at her, she didn't know.

Oh, wait. Yes, she did. It was thanks to the six-foot something pain in the ass standing right next to her, who was currently shouting with the other yahoos and grinning like getting run over by several cubic tons of hoof was his life-long dream. Then again, now that she knew Chris a little better, maybe it was. The man definitely needed therapy.

Considering the fact that she was standing there next to him, it might not hurt to make herself an appointment, either.

Granted, they weren't actually in the middle of the street where the bulls would run. They were on the sidelines. Where it was safe. Not that she believed that for a second. Chris was nearly vibrating with excitement. Charley knew damn well the *only* reason he was on this side of the ridiculously inadequate fence was because of her, and she had no delusions that he'd stay there.

People were shouting and tossing flowers and waving

handkerchiefs, the noise and chaos so great she was about ready to go charging down the street herself to get away from it. Though, she had to admit, the energy was electric.

And contagious.

The sheer magnitude of adrenaline pulsing through the crowd beat through her body. Wound her up. Squeezed the air from her lungs. Sent her heart ricocheting against her ribs like a jackhammer. She hated to admit it, but she could see why Chris would want to be here. What an incredible experience. Even she was starting to get into it.

Then again, the bulls hadn't been released yet.

No sooner had that thought crossed her mind than a pulsing beat reverberated through the street beneath their feet, a steady pounding that echoed through her body and into her chest.

"Here they come!" Chris shouted.

A woman near them screamed, and Charley almost didn't bother looking. Everyone was screaming. But something about the tone was different. Charley glanced over, and her heart crashed to a stop.

The woman was trying to push through the last few people in front of her, her arm reaching out toward her child. The little girl, who was probably about two years old, had gotten away from her mother and managed to duck beneath the barriers along the side of the road. She'd been drawn by the flowers that were strewn in the street and was happily gathering an armful of them. She was still close to the fencing, and no one seemed to notice she was on the wrong side.

But Charley knew the exact moment she decided to venture a little farther. She gasped and grabbed Chris's arm, but he'd already seen her and was on the move. He vaulted over the fence and headed for the child at a full run. He managed to grab her and toss her back over the fence to her mother's outstretched arms just as the thundering chaos of the bulls rounded the corner and headed right for him.

He didn't have time to get back over the fence, though he did pause long enough to give Charley an exultant grin before he turned tail and hauled ass.

"Chris!" she shouted, her voice getting lost in the sea of shouts and cheers from the crowd around her.

She waited until the bulls had passed by, which took almost no time at all. For one, there weren't nearly as many as she'd imagined. In the movies, it always looked like a massive herd, but in reality, there were maybe only a half dozen or so. But the ones who were there were huge, terrifying, and charging down anyone in their path.

Once they passed, she ducked under the fence and took off after them, hoping she'd be able to find Chris. Intact and not flattened like a pancake in the middle of the road.

Unfortunately, everyone else wanted to get in on the action as well and were running alongside her. How she was going to find him in this crowd, she had no idea. She had her phone on her, so she wasn't worried about getting lost. She could call Chris—assuming he and his phone hadn't been trampled—or, failing that, she could make her way back to the house where they were staying.

But worry for Chris grew with every moment she didn't see him. Her eyes scanned both sides of the street, lingering on any groups of people who looked like they might be treating those who'd been injured. No luck.

She finally stopped running and kept going at a brisk walk. She wasn't sure how far the bull run route went, but she didn't want to go too far. There was a huge chance she'd already passed him.

She finally decided to turn back but caught sight of a small group of people standing around a grinning blond man who sat on the ground cradling a bloodstained arm.

Her heart dropped into her shoes, and she hurried over.

"You're hurt!" she said.

He glanced up at her in surprise, and then that charming grin broke out again. "Only a scratch, nothing to worry about."

She crouched down next to him, reaching out for his arm. "Then why are you sitting in the middle of the road?"

"I'm not," he said. "I'm on the side of the road."

She rolled her eyes and muttered, "Smart-ass," low enough he wouldn't hear. Though apparently not low enough because he broke out in a laugh.

"I promise, it's nothing," he said, holding his arm out to her. "See? Fully mobile and everything."

There wasn't much she could do about it just then. Someone had done a decent job of bandaging it, though a small line of blood was seeping through the gauze.

"You're lucky that's all that happened. I can't believe you let a pack of rabid bulls chase you down."

He laughed again. "Hardly a pack. And I can assure you, none of them were rabid."

"That you know of," she muttered.

He let her help him up and then looped his good arm around her shoulders. "It's not like I had much of a choice. I couldn't let that girl get trampled, and the bulls weren't going to wait for me to get back on the other side of the fence."

She took a deep breath and put her arm around his waist. He might insist he was okay, but he leaned on her pretty heavily. He did have a point, though. By the time he'd gotten the girl to safety, the bulls had been bearing down on him. And in the meantime, he'd saved that little girl. The glowing ball of warmth in her heart that had Chris's name on it grew a few more sizes.

"Come on, Superman. Let's get you back home and I'll check on that arm of yours."

• • •

They'd made it back to the house they were staying at and sat sprawled on the living room floor surrounded by first aid supplies.

He much preferred having his arm wrapped around her while she "helped" him walk down the street than having her dab at the angry scratch on his arm. But it was a small price to pay for what had been an exhilarating morning. The fact that the bulls had almost nothing to do with the invigorating energy running through him was something he didn't want to examine too closely.

"Why do you do this?" Charley asked, tossing a bloody gauze pad into the growing pile and picking up an oversize bandage.

He frowned. "Do what? Live my life?"

"Live it like this! Your poor mother must sit by the phone every day terrified she's going to get a call from some hospital somewhere." She smoothed the bandage onto his arm, her movements gentle despite the note of hardness in her voice.

"Leave my mother out of it," he said, trying to tamp back the rush of irritation that her words triggered. That the anger stemmed from her hitting a little too close to the mark wasn't something he wanted to examine too closely.

"I'm sorry. But I don't get it."

"What should I be doing? Sitting in some dark corner somewhere, wrapped up in a fluffy blanket and reading about other people's adventures when I could be out having my own?"

"First of all, everyone loves being wrapped up in fluffy blankets so don't go there, and don't knock curling up with a book. If more people read every now and then, this world would be a lot better off."

His lips twitched, more at the sudden vision he had of her

bundled up on her couch looking insanely adorable than at what she said. "Point taken. My apologies."

"Second of all," she continued as if he hadn't spoken, "it's possible to have adventures without trying to kill yourself every time you step out the door."

"Agreed. And only a crazy person would refer to whitewater rafting and ziplining as trying to kill yourself. They are perfectly safe activities that millions of people enjoy and participate in every year. More people are killed from carbon monoxide poisoning from staying at home curled up in bed than from ziplining."

She folded her arms, her face screwed up into a mixture of frustration and anger that he could relate to all too well.

"And running with the bulls? Or running away from a herd of agitated two-ton animals, I should say?"

Yeah, that one was a little harder to argue, though really, tradition or no, they wouldn't keep doing it if it were all that dangerous.

"Why are we even having this conversation?" he asked. "If you don't like how I live my life, then record it on that little tablet of yours that has probably damned me a thousand times over already and go back to your safe little office."

She glared at him but, again, didn't say anything.

He shook his head. "Why did you come on this trip?"

She blinked at that, a flash of surprise crossing her face. "What do you mean, why did I come? Izzy suggested it, and since you're her friend, I thought I'd do you the favor of trying to get a more accurate look at your life. It's not my fault your life is even worse than I'd thought."

He shook his head again. "Not buying it. In fact, I'm kind of surprised your company allowed it. I doubt you follow many clients around like this. Maybe I should call and ask who's making these decisions, because they should definitely get a demotion."

"No!" Her face drained of color except for two bright red spots on her cheeks, and she looked like she'd knock the phone out of his hand if he tried to use it.

Okay. He'd been kidding, but that reaction was a bit extreme.

She made a visible effort to rein it in and went back to fiddling with the first aid supplies on the floor. "I made the decision so there's really no one to complain to but me." She gave him a vague smile.

"You could have said no."

"You've met Izzy, right?"

He chuckled. "She's good at getting her way, I'll give you that. But you still could have said no. It is a…highly unusual, if not downright inappropriate, set of circumstances."

"That's what I said!"

He lifted his eyebrows again. "Yet here you are."

"Izzy made a good case for why inappropriate was a bit of an exaggeration. Business trips *do* happen all the time. Besides, if you thought it was inappropriate too, *you* could have said no," she said, though that faint blush he was beginning to love stole across her cheeks again.

"I did. But you've met Izzy."

Charley snorted. "I'm starting to sense a theme here."

"You still haven't answered my question," he said. "You've said a hundred times that you could've just done the evaluation from home. In fact, when we met for dinner, you said you were almost done. So why bother coming all this way if you were just planning on condemning me anyway? And don't blame it on Izzy."

She took a deep breath and blew it out. "I'm not sure, okay? I knew it would probably be a disaster. But I thought it could be kind of fun. Unlike you, I can't just jet off to any part of the world I want to at a moment's notice. It was a once-in-a-lifetime opportunity, and I didn't want to regret not going.

And, yes, Izzy. You can't take her out of the equation when she's 90 percent of it. She's your friend, and I know you were doing her a favor choosing me for the job because I'm her cousin. So, while I have no intention of giving you any special treatment where the assessment is involved, it would've still been nice to be able to recommend you, so when Izzy suggested the trip…" She shrugged. "I don't know. I guess it was a straw I grasped at to try and reach the outcome everyone wanted."

He nodded. "Fair enough."

"You never answered my question, either," she said.

"Which was?"

"Why do you do this? Why flirt with danger? And don't give me more of the book-hating BS. What makes a person like you crave the adrenaline rush so bad they'd jeopardize everything?"

He sighed and ran his hand through his hair. He couldn't really refuse to answer after he badgered her into answering his questions. He leaned back against the couch behind him and stretched out his legs, crossing his ankles. He kept his eyes on his feet. Finally, he shrugged and decided to just tell her the truth.

"It probably sounds lame, but I made a vow to myself when I was ten years old that I'd always live life to the fullest. And I'd hate to let myself down," he said with a small smile.

"You decided that at ten years old? That's a pretty mature outlook." She tilted her head to the side, obviously wanting more.

"I was born two months early. Spent seven weeks in the neo-natal intensive care unit. Spent another three months after coming home on an oxygen tank. I walked late, talked late, and didn't catch up to the other kids size-wise until around fourth grade. Despite all that, I was pretty healthy, except for slightly weaker than normal lungs. I didn't ever go full-blown asthma or anything, but if I got a cold, it went straight to croup or something worse. I spent every winter barking like a seal and wheezing to catch my breath when 'normal' kids would just shrug off a regular cold.

"It made my mom a little over-protective of me, which was understandable. She always said she almost lost me as a baby, so she was determined to make sure I made it through childhood okay."

He smiled again. "I love my mom. She's great. But as a kid…it was hard to take. She wouldn't let me join Little League or go outside without at least three layers on. She even tried to make me wear a mask to school when there would be the usual school breakouts of some illness. When I was ten years old, I finally talked her into letting me join the soccer team. She figured that one would be the safest since it was a no contact sport and there were no rock-hard balls flying around."

He laughed. "She figured out that wasn't the case pretty quick when I came home with my first concussion from the ball slamming against my head. But I healed up just fine and was actually in better shape because I was out running around instead of hiding out in the house all the time. She loosened up a bit, and I started joining every team I could. I loved it all. Loved the physical exertion, the adrenaline, the intensity of the competition. The first time I stepped on that field was when I promised myself I'd never just sit around watching the world go by again. I was going to be out there in the thick of it. And I have been ever since."

Charley nodded. "I get that. Really, I do. But I still think there's a difference between playing sports, and even doing something like skydiving where you can at least control most aspects of it, and purposely putting yourself in front of a chummed-up shark or pissed-off bull."

He forced himself to meet and hold her gaze, though he

wanted to do anything but. Because he knew she had a point and he really didn't want to admit that.

She stood up and headed toward the door before stopping to look back at him. "All I'm saying is that when you have people who care about you, who are counting on you, purposely putting yourself in harm's way just for the fun of it is kind of a dick move. There are other ways to get your kicks."

She wasn't wrong. Not that she was right, either. She was maybe 60 percent right. Okay, maybe 75 percent.

More importantly, the flush of her cheeks and the passion behind her words made him think that maybe, just maybe, she might be one of the people who cared about him. At least a little. And damn, if that didn't stir up all kinds of emotions he really wasn't sure how to process.

Hope was at the top of that list.

And hope was a dangerous thing.

Chapter Eleven

She couldn't believe she'd talked to him that way.

The guy was her client.

One who could make or break her fledgling career. One she really needed to stay on the good side of because if he decided to call her company to complain, he'd find out it was really her former company, and she hadn't been exactly forthcoming about all that. Really, it shouldn't matter. She was still doing the same job for him. But...she sighed. Of course, it mattered. Or she would have been upfront in the first place.

She needed to tell him. Maybe he wouldn't care. But if he did—and he might, seeing as how his main endgame was getting insured—well, the thought of losing everything she'd worked so hard for sent a shiver through her. Though a healthy dose of anger went with it. It shouldn't matter. She wouldn't do any better of a job if she'd still been at her old company.

In fact, working for them had made it more and more difficult to do an honest, good job. They would've been pressuring her to recommend him no matter what the numbers said. All they cared about was their bottom line. She cared about doing her job to the best of her ability, and she was damn good at it. She was the best at what she did, no matter who she worked for.

She sighed again. She'd tell him. But…maybe not yet.

She stood at the window in her room and gazed out at the incredible landscape spread out before her. They were staying at one of the properties Chris owned so he could check it out, make sure everything was as it should be. If she owned a place like this, she'd never leave. She didn't know if someone was skimming money on maintenance repairs or what. But this property at least was in amazing shape, from what she'd seen. She could happily spend the rest of her life there, surrounded in breathtaking luxury. Chris didn't know how good he had it.

Then again, he probably did, which was why he spent all his time traveling the world and visiting these amazing places. A far cry from her rooted life. Not that she had too many complaints. Sure, it would be fun to be able to jet off to some exotic location whenever she wanted. But she also really loved having an established home. Traveling the world was fun, but there was definitely something to be said for finding a perfect home and planting some roots.

The sun highlighted the sprawling hills outside the small villa outside the city, touching the tiled roofs of the houses nearby. A friend of hers once asked her why she was so obsessed with all things European. She was forever liking posts and pinning pictures of incredibly beautiful buildings and locations from Europe and Russia and other far away locations she never dreamed she'd get to visit.

Honestly, she wasn't sure. The beauty of these places just struck a chord in her that nothing else did. The United States was filled with breathtaking beauty as well. But as she gazed at the ancient castle that sat on the hill in the far distance, she shook her head. The U.S. just didn't have anything that could compare to the ancient beauty European countries could claim.

A knock sounded at her door, and she told Chris to enter without bothering to take her eyes off the view.

He joined her at the window, and she tried to resist the urge to inhale deeply as the slight breeze from the window blew that manly scent that was uniquely *him* in her direction.

"Beautiful, isn't it?" she said.

"Breathtaking."

She glanced over at him, her heart thumping in her chest when she realized he wasn't looking out the window, but at her.

Her mouth opened and closed a couple times, but she couldn't dredge up a single response to that.

"Hungry?" he asked, his mouth quirked up with that amusement that never seemed to completely desert him.

"I could eat," she said.

He grinned. "Excellent. Carmen left some of her amazing food this morning when she came in to clean."

"Carmen?"

"My housekeeper. She keeps everything going when I'm not here. Why don't you join me? I've got some ideas on what's going on with the maintenance discrepancies."

She nodded and followed him out to the back patio where he'd set everything up. She sat down, closing her eyes and deeply inhaling the tantalizing aroma of Carmen's cooking.

Her stomach audibly rumbled, and he laughed, especially when she covered her flaming cheeks with her hands. It wasn't bad enough that she was always embarrassing herself. Now her body had to chime in and help make it even worse.

"Guess I'm a little hungrier than I thought," she said.

"Carmen's food will do that to you."

They heaped their plates high with piles of rice, chicken, and beans and dug in. They were silent for several minutes, too busy eating to talk much.

"Oh my God," Charley said, covering her mouth with her hand while she chewed. "This is amazing."

He nodded his agreement and shoved another forkful of marinated meat in his mouth. "I've been tempted more than once to make this my home base just so I can eat like this every day."

"Well, if you want a full-time house sitter, you let me know."

He smiled. "I'll keep that in mind."

Her stomach flipped at the flirtatious look in his eyes, and she suddenly wasn't nearly as hungry as she had been a few minutes ago.

"Speaking of house sitters," she said, taking a sip of her wine before turning back to her plate, "what ideas did you have regarding all the discrepancies?"

"Ah. Well, I have a manager who oversees several of my properties. Many of the ones, in fact, that I've been concerned about. There have been some personnel changes lately, and I wasn't sure who was managing some of these properties. He's supposed to have several people under him taking care of various locations."

"And he's been making some personnel cutbacks and taking care of everything himself?"

Chris shrugged. "From what I can tell, yes. One of the managers under him left with no notice a few months ago. And the other apparently went over his head last week and emailed my office about reports he's sent in being ignored or mishandled."

"Well, that doesn't sound good."

He nodded. "Tenants are supposed to contact the manager in charge if there are any problems, and if it's something that needs attention, the head manager is notified so he can take care of whatever issues come up. If it's something abnormal, then he contacts me. But for regular maintenance-type stuff, he's supposed to take care of it. And he has a company credit card to pay for expenses."

"Ah," she said, nodding with understanding. "Let me guess. There's been an unusual number of repairs needed on multiple properties and unusually high charges made on the card in order to supposedly take care of these issues."

"Right," he said, taking a sip of his wine. "And these complaints were never brought to my attention for the most part. I've also never seen a bad review posted to the website or on Yelp or any other site. In fact, all the reviews that have been posted have been glowing recommendations. Generally, if someone has an issue, even if that issue is handled, they mention it."

"Right," she said. "Like—when we arrived, the hot tub was broken, but one call to the manager had it up and running in no time. Four stars."

"Exactly. But there hasn't been anything like that. And with the repairs that have been supposedly needed, I'd expect to hear something about it. Instead, all I've seen are his notes from when the tenants supposedly contacted him."

"Hmm. It does sound suspicious. Is this one of the problem properties?"

He nodded. "According to Juan, the French doors were sticking so badly they were almost unusable, and the hot tub's jets were damaged when a tree limb fell in it, and the repairs were going to cost so much it would be cheaper to just buy a new hot tub. Which he supposedly did."

Charley glanced to the other side of the patio where the hot tub bubbled away happily, waiting for them to climb in. "Is that the new one?"

Chris shook his head. "Juan said he had a new one

installed, but it's the same one that was here before."

"How can you be sure?"

He stood up and held out his hand to her. She hesitated for just a second and then took it, hoping her hand wouldn't tremble when she slipped it into his. Really, there was nothing sexual at all about the gesture, yet the feel of her skin against his sent a fine tremor up her spine.

Luckily, he didn't seem to notice anything, although his hand did grip hers a bit tighter. He led her over to the backside of the hot tub and pointed to a small scratch in the wood. "That happened when we first had it installed two years ago. One of the delivery guys banged into the wall while they were moving it. Yet there is a charge on the company card for a state of the art, brand new hot tub, purchased a week ago. A hot tub Juan told me was installed here."

"So where's the new hot tub?"

Chris shrugged again. "Good question. At Juan's house maybe? Or maybe he was able to return it for cash. Or never bought it in the first place but was somehow able to forge the receipt. I don't know."

Charley leaned over and trailed her fingers in the water. "So, what are you going to do about it?"

"My accountant is already looking into any purchases Juan made. And it looks like I'm going to have to have a conversation with him."

Charley would not want to be Juan. The look on Chris's face was not one she'd want turned against her.

"That's something I'll deal with later. For now, I think we should focus on relaxing." He sighed, sucking in a deep breath and letting it out again. The tension in him loosened up as he exhaled. It was almost like a dog shaking himself and flinging all the water off. Chris seemed to mentally set aside all those problems and refocused on her. It was both enviable and disconcerting.

"Would you like any more?" he asked, gesturing to their plates.

She shook her head. "No thanks. Though there's a good possibility I'll be sneaking into the kitchen in the middle of the night for seconds."

He laughed. "Not if I beat you to them."

"Do you mind if I use the hot tub?"

"Not at all. First, though," he said holding his hand out to her again. She took it with much less hesitation this time. "We're going dancing."

...

Charley's mouth dropped open and she tugged on her hand a little, but Chris didn't let go. He'd figured he might get a little resistance from her, but he was hoping that fun-loving rocker chick from the bar would make an appearance and decide to live a little.

"I'm not sure…"

"Come on. It'll be fun. You can't come to Spain and not go salsa dancing."

Her eyes widened. "Salsa dancing? Isn't that a South American thing?"

"Sure, but it's pretty popular over here also. It's a little different but still a blast."

"I don't have anything to wear. I didn't pack for dancing."

"Not a problem." He led her up the stairs to his room, but she stood rooted at the door. He either had to drag her in or let go of her hand. He contained his inner eye roll but let go.

"Do you have a white blouse or something?" he asked.

She shook her head. "Just T-shirts."

"No problem." He went to his closet and pulled out a white button-up shirt and tossed it at her. "Wear that, only button a few of the buttons in the middle, and tie the bottom in a knot. It'll work great."

Then he pulled a colorful, tasseled shawl off the armchair in the corner. "This should work. Come here."

She remained in the doorway.

"I'm not going to bite. Unless you ask me to."

That got a shy grin out of her, but she still didn't move. So, he went to her, and this time, he pulled her into the room. Then he took the shawl and wrapped it around her waist, leaving one end out. It went around her twice, and he tied it off with the end he'd left sticking out at her waist. "Perfect!"

She raised an eyebrow, and he held up a hand. "Yeah, well, take the jeans off first and add the white shirt. Then it'll be perfect."

She looked down, her fingers running through the tassels. "Not bad. Maybe you missed your calling as a designer."

"You laugh, but I can design the shit out of an evening dress. My sister and I designed a whole collection for a talent show once. Won first place." He grinned at her, still feeling a rush of pride at that accomplishment.

"I'm going to need to see pictures of that."

"Done. But first, go change." He turned her around and shooed her out of the room so he could change himself. He couldn't wait to get her on the dance floor.

They met back in the hallway ten minutes later. She'd left her hair down, and it cascaded around her shoulders in a fluffy riot of waves that had him itching to sink his fingers into it. And he'd been right about the outfit. The shawl hugged her curves like it had been made for them and the white shirt… His mouth turned into a dried-out wasteland, and he forced a swallow.

It covered her, but the buttons she'd left undone gaped when she moved, showing him a tantalizing peek of cleavage. She'd rolled the sleeves up to her elbows, and a tiny hint of her belly showed every now and then. The knowledge that it was *his* shirt she wore sent an already stellar outfit off the charts. A sudden vision of her wearing nothing but that shirt, her hair rumpled from a night in his bed, had his head spinning.

He started to rethink the whole salsa dancing thing. It was something he always did when he was at this particular house. There was a club not too far away that he loved. And it had been a long day. He wanted to blow off some steam and see if Ms. All About the Numbers could cut loose and have a little fun again. That glimpse of her rocking out on stage had whetted his appetite for more.

Not that he didn't enjoy her company when she didn't have a guitar in her hands. He was actually surprised at how much he did, given their different philosophies on life and behavior in general. Still, a night out on the town would do them both some good.

At least, that had been his thinking. Now...he was more than a little afraid it might lead to trouble. Normally, he was down for a good dose of trouble. But he wasn't sure he could handle the kind of trouble she'd bring.

Then again, he'd never been one to back down from a challenge.

"Is this okay?" she asked, a note of anxiety in her voice.

He realized he'd been standing there just staring at her for several moments and tried to shake off the daze she'd put him in.

"Perfection," he said.

Her slow, sultry smile triggered an endorphin rush like he'd never felt before. Better than skydiving. He could so easily become addicted to it. To her.

Oh yeah. Challenge accepted.

Chapter Twelve

The warmth that flooded through Charley at that single word damn near curled her toes. How could one little word—and a smolder that would burn down a brick house—make her want to toss out every rule she'd ever made for herself?

She wasn't generally a go-out-dancing type girl. But after the excitement of the bull run, she had a lot of pent-up adrenaline that needed an outlet. Getting it out on the dance floor was far preferable to a few other ways she could think of to burn off some steam. Well, the consequences were preferable, anyway. A few turns on the dance floor wouldn't destroy her career like a couple other energetic options that came to mind.

Her gaze took in Chris again, raking him over from his artfully tousled hair, down his broad shoulders and muscular chest that strained the ultra-soft T-shirt he wore, down to the slacks that hung from his hips, clinging just enough to outline his well-sculpted ass.

Dayum. Might be worth ruining a career or two over.

She closed her eyes. It only helped a little. But enough that she could function again. Her reaction to him was disturbing on a level she'd never experienced before. Seriously, what the hell? He was just a guy. One she didn't particularly care for. Well, one she didn't agree with on just about everything. She was actually growing kind of fond of the crazy man.

"Ready?" he asked.

She opened her eyes, took a deep breath, and nodded. "Let's go."

They were only in the club about two minutes before she realized what a mistake this might have been. She'd seen salsa dancing before. On *Dancing with the Stars*. It had looked cool. Fun. Sexy, yeah, but in an artful way. A way that took on a whole new meaning when Chris wrapped a hand around her waist and dragged her to him, plastering their bodies together with one hand pressed against the small of her back and the other holding her hand above their heads.

Whooo boy. There was a good possibility she was about to have a stroke and they hadn't even started dancing yet.

"I don't know how to salsa dance," she said, leaning closer so he could hear her over the music and roar of the dancers.

He smiled down at her, sending her stomach into another tailspin.

"There's nothing to it. Just follow my lead and let your body move with the music."

Oh, sure. People who knew what they were doing always made it sound like it was so easy.

She glanced at the people around them. Every one of them moved like they'd been professional dancers their whole lives. There was no way she could move like that.

Before she could back out, Chris gripped her tighter and then bent her over his arm in a quick dip. Her hair whipped forward when he brought her back up and she tossed it back, unconsciously moving with the music.

Chris smiled and took a step to the side, then back, then

to the other side. She followed. His hips pressed against hers, which technically helped her know where to move but for the most part just made her heart race and body burn. The more they moved, though, the more the music and some rhythm she hadn't known she'd possessed took over. She hadn't realized what a sexy instrument the trumpet was until now.

The beat of the congas thrummed through her, and her hips started moving in time with his without much effort on her part.

The end of the first song blended into the second, then the third, and fourth, and still they clung to each other on the dance floor. Twisting. Turning. Dipping. Spinning. Swaying together like they were born to move as one.

She had no idea what she looked like, something that would have consumed her thoughts under normal circumstances. Right then, she didn't care. She'd never had so much fun in her life. She never wanted the night to end. Send the cameras, she was ready for her solo. She had no idea if she was doing the moves right or not. But it felt right. Felt good. She shook her hips, stomped her feet, ran her hands down her body, like she had all the confidence in the world. And for once, she did.

Chris's gaze burned into hers whenever their eyes met. The rest of the time, they roved over her like he had never seen anything so amazing. Whether it was the atmosphere or just some act he was putting on, she couldn't help but believe he meant it. That look in his eyes sent a wave of emotion through her that almost knocked her to her knees. She was somehow renewed, reborn. At that moment, she was the most confident woman in the world. The sexiest. A woman who knew what she wanted and would take it and be damned to anyone in her way.

It was exhilarating. Invigorating. Intoxicating.

And she never wanted it to end. For a brief, crazy

moment, she believed it never would.

But that was so not how her life worked out.

· · ·

Chris was mesmerized. He didn't know what had come over her, but he liked it and wanted it to keep going.

He grabbed her hand and spun her, sending her tassels and hair flying. She laughed and leaned into him, letting her hands run over both of them. Good God, what had he unleashed? And how could he keep it that way?

He wrapped an arm around her waist and bent her over in a deep dip.

And then froze.

Something cracked, and they both heard it. Her eyes flew open, and a strangled gasp squeaked from her throat.

"Are you okay?" he asked, leaning down to talk in her ear.

"I…uh…I don't think so. My back…something definitely cracked or pulled or something."

"Can you stand?"

She hesitated, her breathing shallow. "Maybe. Go slow."

He nodded and gently helped her upright. "How's that?"

She didn't answer for a second, her eyes unfocused like she was trying to listen to whatever clues her body was sending. "Better. I think."

"Okay. Let's get out of here."

She nodded but added, "Slowly."

He wrapped his arm around her waist, drawing her close to his side to give her as much gentle support as he could. He'd pick her up and carry her out except he thought it might hurt her worse. The best he could do was usher her out as fast as possible and make sure their path was clear so she didn't get jostled.

He got her to the car quickly and deposited her as carefully as he could. And for once in his life, he drove the speed limit, avoided all the potholes, and was generally a model driver.

When they got to the house, he helped her out and into the house. Where they both stood in the middle of the room like helpless kittens.

"What would help? Ice? Heat?" Chris had never felt so powerless in his life. He'd just wanted to take her out for a good time and instead he broke her.

"I don't know. It's never done this before. Heat, I think."

"Heat. Okay. I don't know if there's a heating pad here. My mom used to warm a sock full of rice in the microwave. I'm sure there's rice around here somewhere. I just need a sock…Oh! The hot tub. It's nice and hot, and it would take all the pressure off your back."

She nodded slowly. "Yeah. That sounds good. Only…"

"Only what?"

"I don't think I can bend enough to put a suit on."

Oh. Good point. "Just get in like that?"

"In my clothes?"

"Well, you can take them off if you want. I wouldn't mind."

He flashed her his most charming grin, and she snorted. "I think I'll keep them on, thanks."

He'd been kidding, mostly, but it did accomplish one thing—it had brought her smile back. He helped her hobble out to the back patio.

"Actually," she said, "I'm going to lose the skirt."

He froze.

Keep cool. Do not stare. Do not react. She's hurt. She doesn't need you drooling over her like some overly hormonal teenager. Keep. It. Together.

He stood by, afraid to move a muscle, while she reached

down and untied the knot holding her skirt together. She let it drop in a puddle at her feet. He swallowed hard and then let himself look. All the tension immediately released from his body, and he laughed with more than a little relief. The small workout shorts she'd been wearing under the skirt still left little to the imagination, but they covered her to mid-thigh and were very utilitarian. Nothing like the lacy panties he'd been imagining her wearing. Not that he'd been imagining her in her underwear. Okay, maybe just once. Or twice.

She stood watching him, half a smile on her lips. "Scare you for a second there?"

"A little."

She laughed and then winced as the movement pulled at her back. That spurred him into action. He stripped to his boxer briefs and then wrapped an arm around her waist and helped her up the steps and into the tub as gently as he could. She sank beneath the water with a wince, leaning back with a relieved sigh when she was up to her shoulders.

He sat across from her and watched her anxiously. "Better?"

"Oh yeah," she said, closing her eyes and tilting her head back to rest on the rim of the tub.

She sat that way for a few moments and then shifted a few inches to the side, positioning her back in front of one of the jets.

She let out a low moan that echoed through his body and made him very glad the water was too churned up by the jets to allow any visibility of what was going on beneath the surface. Getting in with her had probably been a very poor decision on his part.

They sat silently for several minutes; she let the heat soak into her back while he pretended he wasn't remotely affected by the view in front of him.

Her legs kept bobbing up to the surface and finally floated

close enough that they brushed against him. He wrapped a hand around her ankle, and her eyes flew open. But she made no move to pull her foot from his grasp. He began to massage her feet, and she sighed, tilting her head back and letting her eyes close again. That tiny reaction had his body screaming to do so much more.

"I know I should make you stop," she said. "But honestly, it's been a long day and my body is sore, so I'm just going to sit here and pretend this isn't wildly inappropriate."

He laughed. "How's that working for you?"

She sighed again. "Great so far."

"Well, in that case…turn around."

She cracked an eye open at that. "Excuse me?"

He moved over to her side of the hot tub. "Turn around."

Both eyes now looked at him with suspicion.

"Oh, relax." He took her by the shoulders and turned her away from him. "Here, put your knees on the seat and lean your arms over the edge," he said, positioning her limbs the way he wanted them.

She did as he asked but kept looking at him over her shoulder. "I'm not sure what you have in mind, but I feel the need to warn you that my imagination only stretches so far. A foot rub I can pretend is totally harmless but…"

He laughed again. "I'm going to massage your back. I promise, I have nothing but good intentions."

Intentions, yes. Thoughts, no. Especially when he began massaging his fingers into her back and she rested her head on her arms and arched into him with a soft moan.

He had to close his eyes for a second to shut out the tantalizing sight of her on her knees, poised and ready for him.

Ready for a back rub, *dude. Just a back rub. Cool your jets.*

Easier said than done, however, as he worked his way

down to the small of her back. His thumbs dug into the muscle on either side of her spine, and she tensed up, her breath hissing through her teeth.

"Need me to stop?" he asked, not wanting to hurt her.

"No. Keep going. That's where it hurts the most. The massage is helping, I think. Do you mind if I take the shirt off? It's bunched up around my waist. I think you'll be able to get my muscles better without it."

"Sure," he said, proud his voice didn't end on a squeak.

The shirt *was* bunched up and taking it off *would* allow him better access to her back. The fact that it would reveal more of her silky, smooth skin was a perk he would do his best to ignore.

It took her a few moments to work the wet knot holding the shirt together, and when she finally stripped off the saturated garment, he laughed.

"Were you afraid your entire outfit would disintegrate?" he said, touching the back of the white, form-fitting, midriff-baring tank top she wore.

"Yes, yes I was," she said, smiling at him over her shoulder. "I figured I'd better be prepared for anything."

He chuckled again and returned to work on her back. Between the top and the shorts, she was more covered than a lot of women at the gym he went to—although those women weren't kneeling in front of him begging him for a massage. Covered or no, the woman before him was an absolute goddess, and he prayed his control was strong enough to give her the massage she needed without having to bail for the safety of a cold shower.

She arched under his hands again, her rounded ass almost pushing against him as a breathy little moan escaped her lips. And he was a goner. He needed to stop this, but he kept working his thumbs into the muscles near her spine, his hands squeezing her waist. It took everything he had not to pull her back against him and sink himself balls deep. He ached for her, the burning need growing into a physical pain that only she could soothe.

She gasped under him, pushing up against his hands as he massaged her. His own breath rasped in and out of his lungs, harder than when he'd run from the bulls. He'd barely touched her, and he was on the verge of coming so hard he'd see stars.

He couldn't let this continue. Had to get out of there before he lost what little control he had left. With a ragged sigh, he let go of her. Or tried to. But the moment his grip loosened, Charley grabbed his hands and put them back on her waist, straightening so her back was nearly touching his chest. Then she looked at him over her shoulder, and the raw, burning need in her eyes hit him like a sucker punch to the gut.

She dragged his captive hands up her torso until they covered her breasts, and his fingers closed around them, softly kneading. A raw, lust-filled growl rumbled from his throat, and she sucked in a breath. And then arched into his hands.

Her eyes almost fluttered closed, but she fought to keep her gaze locked with his. Her mouth opened in a soundless gasp, her fingers intertwining with his as they rolled over her tight nipples. Then she rocked back against him, rubbing his hard, aching length against her. "Chris," she whispered.

And he was lost.

Chapter Thirteen

Charley knew she was playing with fire.

There were a million reasons she should jump out of that hot tub and into a cold shower, far away from Chris. Nothing good could come of this. Well…she sucked in another breath as his hands roved a little lower. There was a lot of good that could come of this. But the risks…

His hand trailed up her body until he cupped her face and turned her head enough he could capture her lips. There was nothing soft or careful about the kiss. His tongue tangled with hers, stealing her breath and sending heat racing straight to her core. She wrapped her arm around his neck as best she could and tangled her hands in his hair, keeping him captive while he plundered her mouth.

His free hand dipped below the waistband of her shorts and pressed against her, and she threw her head back, nearly sobbing as one finger slipped inside.

"Easy, baby," he murmured, his lips trailing over her neck.

Easy hell. She grabbed his hand and showed him exactly

what she wanted. She was done counting the risks. Done waiting. Done *wanting*. Yeah, she might feel differently in the morning when a little sanity returned, but right at that moment, she would have gladly sold her soul to keep Chris right where he was.

He chuckled, the sound reverberating through her chest and amping her up even more. And when he slipped a second finger in, the exquisite pressure that had been building exploded, pushing her over the edge. She clung to him, her body trembling with aftershocks that sent tingling pleasure cascading through her.

She hadn't come like that since…maybe ever. And he'd barely touched her.

"God, you're incredible," he said, pressing kisses along her shoulders. "Are you okay?"

"I think okay is the world's biggest understatement."

He laughed. "I meant, how's your back? Still hurt?"

"Oh." She giggled and abruptly clamped her lips down on the sound. She'd never made that sound in her life. Then again, she'd never completely come apart at the seams from five minutes of intense making out, either.

"Yes," she finally managed to say. "It's much better. A little twinge here and there maybe, but better than it was."

"Good." He stood up, putting her eye level with his soaking wet boxer briefs that did absolutely nothing to hide anything. They didn't really before. But saturated with water? Oh, sweet blessed saints.

Before she could lean forward and play out a few fantasies, he took her hand to help her up. He pulled her to him for a hard, fast kiss that had her clinging to him for balance.

"As much as I'd love for you to act on whatever impulse you had going on just then, I don't think I'd last more than thirty seconds with that sweet little mouth on me. And I don't want to come until I'm buried deep inside you."

Oh, she was so down with that.

He helped her out of the hot tub and into his bed, leaving her only briefly to grab a few condoms from the bathroom.

She grinned. "A little ambitious?"

"You have no idea." He dropped them on the bed and quickly put one on before crawling up the bed next to her. He laid on his side and drew her against him, hitching her leg over his hip.

"If your back starts hurting again, you let me know. We'll figure something else out."

She was going to answer, but he reached between them and fit himself against her, and any coherent thoughts fled her mind. Then there was nothing but him. Inside her. Around her. His lips and hands wrought sensations like she'd never felt before. And she didn't think it was because of what he was doing. Other men had touched her. But they weren't *him*.

Every stroke brought her closer to that elusive peak she could never quite reach on her own. That she'd maybe never reached at all. It wasn't just physical. If it had just been physical, she could've given herself over to it. But he was breeching inner walls that she'd had firmly in place for a long time. Letting him in terrified her and thrilled her all at once.

He caressed her back, his lips working gently over hers, kissing and murmuring nonsense to her that somehow meant more than all the false sincerities she'd clung to so hard in the past. He wasn't just in this for a quick night of fun. Every touch seemed to be a promise. Every thrust, every kiss, every brush of his hands and lips broke down her barriers and branded her his.

And when they finally came, screaming each other's names, she let him curl around her, giving herself fully over to him. Whether it was for that one moment or forever, she didn't care. For once in her life, she was going to ignore the risks. Ignore the fear. And let herself be happy, with no strings.

She'd have plenty of time to worry about it later.

. . .

The early morning sun streaming in the window roused Chris from sleep long before he was ready to get up.

Then again, there were plenty of entertaining activities that could be enjoyed in bed. He rolled over and reached for Charley...but found only cool sheets. He frowned and sat up, looking for any sign of her. She definitely wasn't in the room. Or the bathroom.

Faint sounds drifted in from the kitchen, and the empty rumbling of his stomach reminded him of a few other things that needed attending. He yanked on his favorite worn jeans that were laying on the floor and went to find Charley.

The smell of something amazing hit him when he was halfway down the hall, and he picked up the pace. Charley was in the kitchen stirring something in a pan over the stove. She looked up when he entered but wouldn't meet his gaze. Those cheeks of hers flushed pink again, and she looked back down at the pan she held.

He grinned with a rush of pure masculine pride that he was the one who'd put that well-loved and satisfied look on her face. The fact that she still blushed after the things they'd done was unbelievably cute. He came up behind her and wrapped his arms around her waist, burying his face in her neck. He planted kisses along her shoulder and neck until he reached the soft skin behind her ear. She shivered in his arms and melted back against him for a second before standing up straight again.

She twisted out of his grasp, shaking her head. "Wait, Chris. I think we need—"

"More of this?" he asked, hauling her back to him so he

could give her a proper good morning kiss.

Once again, she responded, her body pressing against his before she pulled away. She put a hand on his chest when he tried to pull her back.

"I think we should talk about last night," she said.

Her tone suggested he wasn't going to like what she had to say, and for the first time he realized she might not be feeling as euphoric as he.

"Last night was amazing."

"It was," she said with a soft smile.

He reached out to brush a thumb along her cheek, gently so he didn't spook her. Something seemed…off. Why did she keep pulling away? He wanted to touch her. No, more than that. He craved her. Standing so close and not touching her felt so wrong. He couldn't be the only one feeling that way.

"But," she said, stepping back again.

A cold ball of ice dropped into his stomach. "But what?"

She took a deep breath but still wouldn't meet his gaze. "I just…I think…I think it was probably a mistake."

The ice spread to his veins. "What do you mean? Did you not want…"

"No, I did. I absolutely did. And it was…incredible."

Her breath hitched a little on that last word, and he cocked an eyebrow, waiting for her to continue.

"I…it's probably not something that should happen again, is all."

His second eyebrow joined the first. "And why's that?"

"Because…"

She sighed, and he smiled again.

"We're two consenting adults who had an amazing time together. Personally, I think turning it into a one-and-done would be a crying shame. Why shouldn't we keep having a good time?"

"Because," she said, throwing her hands up, "what

happens next?"

His forehead creased at that, and he looked at her a little more closely. "What do you mean?"

"Oh, get the suspicious look off your face."

He blinked in surprise, not realizing he'd had a suspicious look on his face. Though he had been suspicious of what was about to come out of her mouth. Was this the part where she said she didn't feel right being with him unless they were married or committed or something? That's what most women he'd been with did. Tried to lock it down as fast as possible.

He had to admit if anyone seemed like they were trying to lock it down in their current situation, it was him. He was the one trying to get things going again, while she was practically running around the kitchen trying to get away from him.

He jammed a hand through his hair and sighed. "Why don't we sit down, eat whatever it is that you made there, and we can talk? Okay?"

She glanced down at the pan in her hand, her eyes slightly round with surprise as if she'd forgotten it was there.

"Okay. We can do that."

He nodded and then went through the kitchen, gathering up plates and utensils, some fresh juice from the fridge, and some glasses. In the meantime, Charley carted over bacon, sausage, an amazing-looking frittata, and some sticky buns from the bakery down the road.

"How long have you been up?" he asked.

"A while."

"Uh huh." He sat down and stuffed half a sticky bun in his mouth. "Okay," he said, once his mouth was mostly clear. "Lay it on me. What's eating at you?"

She closed her eyes and took a deep breath. Then blurted it all out like she was afraid she'd chicken out if she didn't hurry and say it. "I don't want you thinking that last night only happened because I'm trying to get on your good side."

He frowned slightly at that. "Wouldn't that be my reasoning for last night? Getting on your good side so you'd give me your recommendation?"

"Well, yeah, that's the other point I was going to make. How do I know that wasn't why?"

His eyes narrowed at that. "Do you really think that? Because that would be a seriously dick move, and despite my winning demeanor, I'm not usually a total asshole. I wouldn't sleep with you to get your stamp of approval."

"No, I didn't think that's what you were doing. Not really. And that's certainly not why I slept with you."

"And I never would have thought you did."

"Right. But everyone else will."

He frowned again. "What are you talking about?"

Charley sighed and put her fork down. "I don't want to get a reputation for sleeping with my clients. And I don't want people thinking I slept my way to the top."

"Well, it's not like I was planning on having a press conference to announce what happened, but even if word does get out, why do you care what people think? Screw them."

"Easy for you to say. All you'll get is a few high fives and dirty innuendos. But I'll lose any sort of credibility or respect I've managed to claw out for myself. And let me tell you, there hasn't been much so far."

He opened his mouth to argue but then shut it, embarrassed he'd never really thought about how it might look. She wasn't wrong. Most of his board would probably think his sleeping with his assessor was a great strategy on his part to get a good result. And they'd definitely think way less of her for the same thing.

He sighed and jammed his fingers through his hair then leaned over so he could take her hand in his.

"Okay, then. So how about this? We don't tell anyone. It's no one's damn business anyway. I'm not sleeping with you to get a recommendation—for my company, anyway. You want to recommend me on my other skills, I'm down with that."

She choked a little on the coffee she'd sipped, and he grinned. "And you are not sleeping with me for my contacts or to get ahead in your company or any other reason except that I'm that fucking hot and you just couldn't resist."

"You're not far off," she said quietly. Her teeth sank into a strawberry, and he sucked in a breath as if she'd sunk her teeth into him.

"Right. Okay then." He stood, pulled her to her feet, and carried her fireman style back to the bedroom.

"What are you doing?" she asked, though there was laughter in her voice.

He slapped her butt. "Making sure we're on the same page about what's going on. I thought a visual demonstration of our mutual understanding would be best."

He dropped her on the bed and crawled over her. She reached up and let her nails lightly drag across his chest as he moved higher, and he shivered under her touch.

"This might have to go in my report," she murmured, lifting her head so she could flick a tongue across his nipple.

"Fuck," he groaned. "You can put anything you want in that report as long as you do that again."

The sultry laugh that echoed from her throat had him threading his fingers through her hair so he could capture her mouth.

He didn't know what was going between the two of them. Didn't want to try and put a label on it, not just yet. All he knew was he'd agree to anything she wanted as long as she'd keep kissing him like she was now. All tongue and lips and teeth and unbridled passion. He didn't know her story. Yet. But he'd never met anyone so in need of letting loose in his life. The woman had uptight down to a science. And he knew just how to make her unravel.

He slipped a finger between her legs and smiled when she arched into his hand. "That's right, baby," he said, giving her a taste of what he planned to do to her. "I'm going to make you come at least twice. And then we'll go do something really fun."

Her eyes fluttered back. He laughed and then settled between her legs to drive his point home.

Chapter Fourteen

Charley stood at the top of the platform and risked a peek over the edge even though she already knew how far down the drop was. Her stomach flipped, and she stepped back as far as she could.

When Chris had woken up the morning before with the announcement that they were headed to Fiji because, as he put it, *why not*, Charley had envisioned naps on the beach and splashing in the gorgeous ocean. Not dangling above the jungle while she clung to a flimsy-looking rope. Then again, she was with Chris, so she shouldn't have been surprised. Naps on the beach weren't really his thing. Flirting with death for a few minutes of adrenaline rush, now *that* was his thing.

The guy running the place came over and started strapping her into an intricate harness she'd never get out of herself. On the one hand, it seemed pretty secure. On the other, that meant exactly squat if the zipline she was on broke. It just meant she'd die strapped in instead of flying free.

"Why are we doing this again?" she asked Chris, who was all harnessed up and standing cool as a margarita at the edge waiting for her.

"Because it's fun," he said, his voice the same tone someone would use for a toddler.

She raised an eyebrow, and he laughed. "Give it a chance. It's totally freeing. Not as great as skydiving, but I figured I'd better start you out slow."

All the blood drained from her face at just the mention of skydiving, and she gripped the ropes she was strapped to until her knuckles turned white.

"Relax, Chuck," Chris said with another laugh. "I promise, it's amazing."

"Chuck, huh?"

"Yeah, it's cute. Why should Izzy get all the fun?" He winked at her, and Charley laughed despite the fine haze of fear saturating her very being.

The zipline guy gave them the thumbs up. "You're all ready."

No, she wasn't. Not even close. Ohhh, she should so not be doing this. Her risk-o-meter was going off big time. Likelihood of death—1,000 percent.

Yet still she eased up to the edge of the platform, her blood thundering in her ears.

"You good?" Chris asked, still smiling but with a crease of concern crinkling his forehead. "You really don't have to do this if you don't want to. Might want to decide quick, though."

She shook her head and gripped her ropes tighter. "No, I'm already up here and suited up and everything. I just… need a second."

"It's probably better if you're surprised. Close your eyes and just walk. Or let them push you off. That way the anticipation isn't so bad. Like ripping off a bandage. Jumping in the pool. Plucking a chin hair."

That one got her attention. "You pluck your chin hairs?"

"No, but I used to watch my nana do it, and it looked painful."

"Ah," she said with a nod.

"Eyebrow hairs are another matter."

That startled another laugh out of her. She shook her head and then took a deep breath. She could do this. One step further and she'd be soaring. Theoretically, it sounded wonderful, which was how he'd gotten her up there in the first place. Actually taking the leap was another matter entirely.

And boy if that whole situation didn't feel particularly apt right then.

She took another peek at Chris, at that smile that made her knees weak. The chiseled body that made the rest of her weak. And the charming, witty, kind, and intelligent parts of him. What was she going to do with him? Them? She'd expected a nice little one-night fling. It couldn't be more than that. Except now it seemed like Chris, at least, wanted to make it more. Did she?

A big part of her did. She'd never met anyone like him. He seemed to get her like no one else ever had. And miracle of miracles, he seemed to like her, even though he'd seen the less than perfect version of her that she couldn't seem to keep contained around him. She couldn't lie, even to herself. She was having the time of her life; even if he walked away right then, she'd still consider the trip well worth it. Full of memories that would last her for a lifetime.

But that didn't mean they should try and make this whole thing any more than they, or she at least, had intended.

She was so lost in her thoughts she barely registered the guy behind her was counting down. Until he reached nine and Chris gave her a huge grin and thumbs up. She only had a second to catch her breath before Zippy gave her a little push and off she went.

She screamed until she ran out of breath and then sucked

in a lungful so she could scream some more. But before she could, she caught sight of Chris flying along beside her. His face was alight with joy. She'd never seem him look so happy and…alive. Well, out of bed anyway.

She gripped the ropes she was strapped to tighter and dared a look around as she zoomed above the trees. From way up there, she could see for miles. The stunning, breathtaking beauty was unreal. It looked more like a painting. Or some CGI special effects. The sheer amounts of greenery with the sparkling ocean in the distance took her breath away, and she was flying up above it all.

Chris was watching her, and when their eyes met, his smile grew even wider.

"Isn't this amazing?" he called out.

She laughed. "Yes!"

"Woohoo!" His voice rang out over the landscape. He opened his arms wide and tilted his head back, obviously loving the feeling of flying along in midair.

It was far more exhilarating than Charley had ever dreamed possible. She could almost understand why people went skydiving, if it was anything like ziplining. If zooming through the air on a rope created the kind of adrenaline-pumped sensations she was experiencing, then flying through the air after jumping from a plane must be an out-of-this-world experience.

The adrenaline rush *was* addicting. There she was, not even through with one rush and another already beckoned. And it could keep on beckoning. There was no way she was jumping from a perfectly good plane. But ziplining…that one she might try again.

The end of the line neared, and the excited euphoria of the whole flying experience changed to a sudden dread of crashing into the landing platform. It didn't help when they jerked her to a stop several feet from the pad. She knew it was going to happen since they had to slow their arrival or they really would crash right into the pad. But the jolt when she was still dangling hundreds of feet in the air was a stomach-dropping experience.

She renewed her grip on her cables, though the death grip she already had going on was going to leave permanent half-moon circles in her palms. Chris, on the other hand, was completely chillaxing. Legs dangling in the breeze. He ran a hand over his face and held his arms out again, looking at her with a grin that melted her heart.

"Didn't I tell you that would be amazing?"

She laughed, his happiness and enthusiasm contagious.

"I admit, it was pretty cool."

They towed her in first, and while she actually had enjoyed herself, in an omg-that-was-awesome-glad-I-didn't-die kind of way, having her feet back on solid ground was heavenly. Well, solid platform anyway. The ground was still much too far away, but better.

There seemed to be an issue with Chris's line, though. The two guys who were running this end of the platform stood near where the line was towed in, a flurry of Spanish going between them too quickly for her to follow.

Chris didn't look overly concerned, merely curious as he watched them trying to work out whatever kink was leaving him dangling in midair. His line jerked several times, rocking him to and fro. And every time a sudden jolt sent him swinging, Charley's heart would lodge in her throat.

They finally got things fixed and towed him the rest of the way in. Once they got all his gear off him, he came toward her with open arms and huge grin.

She flung herself around his neck. "Okay, that freaked me out."

He pulled back, his smile dimmed a bit. "I thought you had fun. It looked like you were enjoying yourself."

"I did. The actual ziplining was amazing. Oh my God, you could see for miles, and the view was incredible."

"And the flying?"

"The flying I liked slightly less," she said, holding up a finger to ward off whatever smart-ass remark he was about to make. "But it was kind of fun."

"Only kind of, huh?"

"Fun in the way that a roller coaster or haunted house is fun."

"Right!"

She snorted. "I think maybe fun is the wrong word. Exhilarating. It was definitely exhilarating."

"Hmm," he said, leaning in for a kiss. "You weren't too scared, were you?"

"You'd have to define *too scared*."

He laughed again. "You just seem a little...clingy, that's all."

"Oh, really?"

She tried to pull away, but he kept her locked in his arms. "I didn't say I minded clingy."

Before she could argue with him further, he captured her mouth in a kiss that did more to wreck her equilibrium than the whole ziplining experience. Normally, she'd want to move somewhere a little more private instead of making out in front of two total strangers. But at that moment, she didn't care who was watching them. She'd make out in front of the Pope himself as long as Chris's lips stayed on hers.

"Come on," he said, breaking away from her and taking her hand.

"Where are we going?"

He pulled her along behind him down the winding steps of the platform and marched straight to where their car was parked.

"Chris," she said, laughing, having to run to keep up with

him. "Where are we going?"

"Somewhere I can get you alone so I can rip those little shorts off you and show you some real fun."

Her breath caught in her throat, and she gripped his hand, her blood roaring through her for a whole different reason now.

They made it back to the car and jumped inside, Chris starting it and backing out of there like the cops were on his tail.

"Where are we going?" she asked again, leaning over to kiss his neck.

He groaned and punched the gas. She gasped, though she was half laughing as well, residual excitement from the zipline and sheer, hard lust pulsing through her so hard her head swam.

"There's a small beach up the road. It's quiet, private. And close."

"A beach?"

Beaches, despite how they were depicted in romance novels and films, were not the sexiest place to get it on. Beaches had sand. Sand was abrasive and sticky. And got everywhere.

He chuckled, obviously reading her thoughts. "No worries. I've got a few ideas. I know sand isn't ideal, but the beach is secluded, and I figured you'd prefer not to have an audience while I make you scream my name."

Her cheeks flamed hot, but his blunt language sent a bolt of electricity straight to her core. She bit her lip, her breath already coming out in short pants, and he hadn't even touched her yet.

The road to the beach was more of a windy, unmarked path barely cleared of vegetation. If they hadn't been in a tough Jeep that had obviously seen its fair share of off-roading, they'd never have made it down to the shore. And he was right when he said it was small and secluded. It was barely more than a small strip of sand surrounded by jungle vegetation on all sides. It was perfect.

Chris threw the car into park and moved his seat back as far as it could go.

"Come here," he said, unbuttoning his shorts.

She grabbed her purse and threw him a condom she'd stashed in there. He grinned at her and rolled it on while she shimmied out of her shorts and panties. Then he pulled her onto his lap. She straddled him, laughing when her legs bumped against the doors and console.

Her laugh cut off abruptly when he angled himself against her and plunged inside. She curled around him, bracing her hands on the back of his seat. She tried moving with him and banged against the steering wheel.

They laughed again until he grasped her hips and helped guide her as he thrust deeper.

It didn't take long, only a few more thrusts before she was shuddering around him. He was right behind her, pressing his face into her neck as he moaned his release.

They held each other for a few more moments while the aftershocks wore off. Then she laughed and leaned down for a kiss.

"That was a first for me."

"Hmm," he said, giving her butt a soft slap and a squeeze. "Well, you're a total natural. I'll have to buy a few more cars just so we can christen them."

"Ha! You do that," she said, though she belatedly realized he could, and probably would, do exactly that.

"Let's go for a swim," he said, giving her a quick kiss as she climbed off his lap.

"But we didn't bring suits."

He laughed. "There's no one here but you and me."

Her mouth dropped open, and he winked at her. "If

you're uncomfortable with that, your bra and panties should suffice. They cover you more than most bikinis."

This was true. And she would feel more comfortable with something on.

Chris, however, had no such hang ups. He strode proud and butt naked right into the surf. Charley just shook her head, though she smiled, admiring the spectacular view.

How was she ever going to make herself walk away from him when all this was done?

Chapter Fifteen

Charley snuggled closer to Chris, listening to his heartbeat beneath her ear. She'd been awake for a while, but she didn't want to disturb him if she got up. Though the bathroom was calling her name so she might have to see if she could wiggle out.

She finally managed to skootch out and pulled on the T-shirt he'd ripped off last night, then tiptoed across the floor, happy she hadn't woken him.

"Hurry back," he said with that still-asleep gravel in his voice.

She laughed and hurried into the bathroom. Once in there, though, her amusement faded. The guilt over her lie about her job had been eating at her from the start. But since they had...hooked up or gotten together or whatever they hell they were doing, it had been growing—to the point she couldn't ignore it anymore. She had to tell him.

He might not care. Truly, he didn't seem the type to worry overly much about company names or big corporations. In fact, he might prefer she was on her own, a new, small company.

Or at least he might have been good with it had she been upfront in the first place. Instead, she'd lied. Well, not lied exactly. But she hadn't been honest about her parting ways with her company. And while it might not matter to Chris, it probably would matter to his board, and the insurance company, who were the ones she really had to answer to anyway. She didn't think Chris would be the brunt of any fallout if it were a big issue. But what if he was? What if she was screwing up everything for him because of her deception?

Which led to another problem. He said he'd never have thought she was sleeping with him to get ahead. But that might change when he found out she wasn't some well-respected member of a large company but an imposter who'd been fired from her company and was now trying to make a name for herself, something she could do if she landed Chris's account and did well. Would he still believe her interest in him was purely personal and not professional? Because it sounded shady even to her, and she knew the truth.

She propped her elbows on her knees and put her head in her hands. How did she go from fledgling risk assessor on a business trip to a sort of girlfriend of her billionaire client hiding out in his bathroom?

She didn't know how she'd reached this point, but she'd have to get off the toilet and face it at some point. And she'd rather fess up now and let him hear it from her rather than hearing it from someone else. The thought of destroying the perfect little bubble of happiness they'd created for themselves ripped a hole in her heart. But it would be so much worse if she waited.

She sighed and went to wash her hands. Some cold water on her face and a quick hair fluff helped, too. Might as well try and look halfway decent before she went out and ruined what could have been the best thing to ever happen to her.

The moment she opened the door, she knew it was too late.

Chris sat on the edge of the bed, the sheet barely covering his lap. But she couldn't enjoy the mouthwatering view he presented, because he had his phone to his ear. And whoever was on the other side was giving him bad news about her, judging by the betrayed and angry look he gave her.

Charley sighed, swallowing past the sudden lump in her throat. She went into the closet and pulled on a pair of jeans. She didn't want to be sitting there half naked when the fight that was about to happen went down. Not that it would be much of a fight, really. She was in the wrong.

Then she went back out and sat on the chair by the window and waited for him to hang up. She didn't have to wait long.

He dropped his phone on the bed beside him and looked over at her. "That was my assistant. She had an interesting conversation with Phosphorus Assessments. Any guesses as to what they said?"

His voice was hard, cold. She'd never heard it like that before. Even when he'd been displeased about something. There was always something…kind, amused about his voice. But not this time. He was truly angry, and he had every right to be.

She took a deep breath and slowly let it out. "I assume she was informing you I no longer work for their company."

He looked at her for a minute, saying nothing, long enough that she wanted to squirm. But she kept it together, barely. She forced herself to meet his gaze, not look away. He seemed to be struggling with how to respond. She didn't blame him. She didn't know how to respond, and she was the one who caused the whole mess.

Finally, he closed his eyes and rubbed his hand over his face. "Why would you lie? Are you even a risk assessor? Was this whole thing some weird, cruel prank that Izzy or my friends set up? I mean, I know they like their practical jokes, but I didn't think they'd ever take it this far," he said, waving his hand to encompass the bed.

She shook her head and sat forward in her chair. "No, I'd never be part of something like that."

"No? Just some elaborate lie that's about to tank my career?"

White-hot guilt stabbed her through the chest, and she had to bite her lip to keep from crying. But she couldn't let him think what he was obviously thinking.

"Chris, I never meant to do any harm, I swear. I *am* a risk assessor. When Phosphorus unfairly let me go, I started my own company. Izzy had already talked to you about me, so we thought…"

"You thought you'd lie so you could keep the job and make a name for yourself with a big name like mine."

She shook her head again, though he wasn't wrong. "I didn't lie. I just…didn't tell you the whole truth."

"Oh, because that's so much better."

He stood up and jammed his fingers through his hair again. He grabbed his pants from the floor and pulled them on. "Why didn't you just tell me? Like you said, Izzy had already talked to me about you. She'd already secured the job for you. So why the lie?"

"I don't know," Charley said, wishing she could sink into the chair and somehow be magically back home before she'd made the stupid decision to follow through with any of this. "We weren't sure the board would go for it, and since you'd already approved me, it shouldn't have mattered because it was still me doing the job for you. I know I don't have the big company behind me, but I'm still really good at my job."

"You don't get it, Charley. I'm not upset because you don't have a company behind you. I'm upset because you weren't honest with me. Because you let things get *this far* without saying a word," he said, gesturing at the bed.

Anger started to burn away the guilt that had been eating at her. "I told you why I wasn't upfront with you, and yeah, it might have been a dumb decision, but we really didn't think it mattered in the long run. And I wanted to tell you. I just could never seem to find the right time. I was actually coming out here to tell you right now, but you were already on the phone."

"Oh, sure, you were going to tell me now. That's convenient, seeing as how I already know." He paced toward the door then turned and paced back. "You know, I'm used to other people pulling this shit. But you I thought I could trust. I'll talk to Izzy later. But…what you and I had…or what I thought we had, anyway…you say that wasn't a part of it all, but how am I ever going to know that for sure?"

Charley stood, anger and indignation flowing through her. "Because I told you so, that's how. Do you really think I'd sleep with you for a job? What kind of person do you think I am?"

Chris shrugged. "It seems I don't know what kind of person you are. I thought I knew, but obviously I was wrong."

"That's bullshit. Nothing about me has changed. Nothing about us or how we are together or what happened between us has anything to do with either of our jobs. I would never use you like that. You know that. You know me."

He just looked at her, the sadness in his eyes twisting like a knife in her gut. "How can I ever trust you now?"

"Well, if I'm able to trust that you weren't with me just to get approved and keep your company—something that's much more likely, by the way—then you should be able to trust that I'm not using you."

He stared at her so long she didn't think he'd ever answer. Finally, he sighed.

"I don't know that I can."

"Right. Fine," Charley said, her heart breaking in a million pieces. She marched for the closet. She had to get out of there. She grabbed her bag from the floor and shoved in whatever clothes she could find that were fast and easy to grab. Her passport was still safely in its hidden pocket inside the bag. She shoved her feet into some sandals and marched back out into the room and straight out the door.

She didn't stop to look at Chris. If she looked at him now, she'd lose it. She kept going until she was out the front door.

He didn't stop her.

Luckily, Lucas was outside cleaning out the car with one of those rolling vacuums.

"Lucas, can you take me to the airport, please?"

He looked up at her, eyes wide with surprise. And then he glanced over her shoulder. Charley looked, too, unable to stop herself from doing so. Her gaze met Chris's, locked with it. He gave a subtle nod of his head, and the last piece of her heart crumbled.

He wasn't going to fight for her. Not even a word.

Lucas put the vacuum to the side and took her bag before opening the car door. She got inside and tried to focus on breathing. Chris hadn't gone back in the house. She could see him out of her peripheral vision, watching the car until they pulled away. Only then did she let her tears fall.

"Are you okay, miss?" Lucas asked.

"Yes. Fine," she said, yanking her phone out of her bag. "I just need to go to the airport please."

He nodded and didn't say another word, for which she was eternally grateful.

She punched in Izzy's contact info and waited for her cousin to pick up. The second she did, Charley unleashed the torrent. The only mostly coherent thing she managed to get out was that she was in Fiji and wanted to go home.

"Wait, Fiji? What are you doing in Fiji?" Izzy asked.

"I don't know! He woke up one morning and said let's go to Fiji, so we went to Fiji. I don't know why. He's crazy. It doesn't matter why we went; I just want to get out of here and go home."

There was nothing but stunned silence on the other end of the phone. Then Izzy said, "Well, damn."

Charley snorted. "That about sums it up."

"What happened?"

Charley took a deep breath and let it out. "It was all going great. I thought we were having fun. And…well, I thought maybe it could be more. But I was feeling guilty over not telling him about my job, so I was going to tell him, but he got a call from his company, and they found out about me and told him before I could, and he got mad because I lied to him. But I was going to tell him, only he didn't believe me, and then we got in whole fight, and I can't blame him for hating me. Even though if I could trust that he wasn't using me, he should be able to trust me. But you should have seen his face. I had to get out of there. I just want to go home, Iz, but I don't have a ticket, and I don't know how much one costs, but I doubt I have it in my account, and I don't know what to do."

"Hey, just breathe, okay?"

Charley took another deep breath and nodded her head, even though she knew Izzy couldn't see her.

"Okay, don't worry. I've got you covered. Tell me what airport you're going to and give me fifteen minutes."

Charley asked Lucas for the info and passed it along to Izzy. And God bless her cousin, but she really did get everything taken care of. By the time she got to the airport, Izzy had her set up with a first-class ticket on the first flight leaving the island. Which, as luck would have it, was soon enough that Charley had to go straight to the gate.

For a few ridiculous minutes, she held out hope Chris

would storm the plane, say he was sorry, tell her he loved her, and they could work it out. But she wasn't surprised when none of that happened. The doors closed, the plane taxied out, and she was on her way back home.

No Chris.

No job.

Almost certainly no career.

And no one to blame for it but herself.

Chapter Sixteen

It took all of three minutes for Chris to regret letting Charley walk out the door. It took longer to get a taxi out to the house to get him to the airport.

He had no idea what he was going to say to her. He was still pissed. He couldn't believe she'd pull something like that. Though...she hadn't been wrong. She was still doing the job she was hired for. True, she'd been fired from the company before she could finish the job, but like she said, he'd only hired that firm so he could get her. So, it shouldn't make a difference. And it didn't, really. Except for the fact that she hadn't told him about it.

Though even that he could understand. It didn't make a difference to him who she worked for. But it almost certainly would have made a difference to his board.

And now...he didn't know what was going to happen. Everything was in turmoil. His board was freaking out. The insurance company was balking. And Charley...Charley wasn't answering her phone.

The taxi pulled up to the airport, and Chris shoved some

money at the driver and then got out, prepared to run. But his phone rang, and he stopped short, holding his breath until he saw that it wasn't Charley, but Izzy.

He thought about ignoring it, but that wouldn't stop Izzy from getting a hold of him if she was really determined.

He answered and put the phone to his ear. "I really can't talk right now, Iz—"

"Good! Then you can just listen. What the hell were you thinking? All that mess with the job and the lie and everything else is all my fault. All of it. I talked her into that; she didn't want to go along with it. And it really shouldn't make that big a difference anyway. And now she's sitting on the plane, crying her eyes out, and—"

"Wait," he said, his heart twisting at the thought of her crying. "She's already on the plane?"

"Yeah. It left ten minutes ago."

Chris released a huge sigh, and the crack in his heart that started when he'd gotten that phone call opened wide.

"Why?" Izzy asked. "Where are you?"

He sat down on a bench beneath a palm tree and leaned his elbow on his knee, head hanging. "At the airport."

"Good!"

He had to hold the phone away from his ear, she squealed so loud.

"Get your ass on the next plane and go get her!"

Part of him wanted to do exactly that. A very big part. But the rest…

"I don't know, Izzy. Maybe it's a sign."

"A sign of what? You being a total and complete coward and letting the best thing that ever happened to you slip out of your life?"

"Wow, Iz, tell me how you really feel."

"I'm not joking, Chris. If you don't go after her, you'll regret it."

He sighed. "Maybe. But maybe it's better if we let the whole thing go."

"How can you say that?"

"Because. We haven't known each other that long, and apparently everything we did have together was based on a lie."

"That's bullshit, and you know it. She didn't lie to you, she just didn't tell you the whole truth, and even that was my fault. She's been wanting to tell you since the beginning, and I bet she probably would have soon even if you hadn't found out."

He didn't tell her Charley had said she was going to tell him that morning. He didn't want to give her any more ammo. Because if he wasn't careful, she would talk him into going after Charley, and the more he thought about it, the more he thought it might be best to just go back to how life had been before her.

Even if that life now seemed like a pointless pit of loneliness.

"And it doesn't matter how long you know someone," Izzy said. "Look at Harrison and Nikki. They barely knew each other too when they first fell in love. When it's the right person, it doesn't take all that long. You're just running scared."

"You're damn right I am! And maybe that means something. The instinct to run isn't always wrong, you know."

Izzy sighed, her frustration palpable, even over the phone. "Well, it's wrong this time."

Chris scrubbed another hand over his face. "Even if I were to forget everything else, all this lie stuff, all the issues with the job and whether or not I can ever trust her again, I still don't think it'll work."

"And why is that?" she asked, her voice full of skepticism.

"We're two different people, Izzy. I like to live life to the fullest. Seize the day and make every moment count."

"Yeah, you're a giant walking cliché, got it. What's that got to do with anything?"

"The woman assesses risk for a living, Iz, which makes someone who was probably cautious to begin with almost certifiably careful. I'm actually amazed I got her to do half the things she did."

"Right. But you did. And from what I heard, she enjoyed every minute. So maybe you aren't so different after all."

"Really? Can you see me spending my life with someone who is so overly cautious about everything that she won't even use a public restroom without completely disinfecting it first? She has a bottle of Lysol in her purse, Izzy. And I spent my last birthday eating bugs in a Taiwanese street market."

"That's not necessarily a bad thing, Chris. You could stand to tone it down a bit, and it sounds like you're already getting her to come out of her little safety bubble and try new things. You have no idea how long I've tried that."

"What is her deal?"

Izzy was quiet for a second. "You should probably ask her."

He snorted. "You think she'll tell me?"

"I don't know. She doesn't like talking about it."

"Right. And I guarantee she'll be less likely to tell me about it now."

Izzy sighed. "Her brother was injured in a car wreck in high school. Charley was driving. She blames herself for what happened to him."

"Is he okay?"

"Mostly," Izzy said. "But he lost an ear and has short-term memory problems. He went from a straight-A student to flunking all his classes. They got him help so he was able to turn things around and graduate, but he still has bad panic attacks. Charley sort of took it on herself to help him out as much as she can. She's always looking for anything in any given situation he's in that might trigger a panic attack so she can head it off."

Chris flinched like someone had punched him in the gut at the thought of Charley having to carry that around her whole life. So much about her made sense now. But that didn't make his feelings about them better. If anything, it made things worse.

"So, she has her reasons for how she is."

"I get that, Izzy, I really do. And I have my reasons for how I am. But that's the problem. Neither one of us are going to change, for good reason. So, how can our lives possibly mesh?"

"Chris…"

"It's okay, Iz." He blew out a long breath. "Just let it go. We're probably better off. Trying to force this will only end up in both of us being hurt worse."

Izzy was quiet for so long that Chris thought she might have hung up. Finally, she sighed. "Do what you gotta do. But for what it's worth, I think you're wrong. You're focusing on the bad stuff, on what went wrong. Maybe you should think about what went right. There must've been something there between you two. I guess you need to figure out if that's worth fighting for or not."

"Yeah. Maybe."

"We're all headed back to New York in the morning. You coming to the poker game Thursday?"

The last thing he wanted was to spend the evening surrounded by his friends and their spouses. It was hard enough to take when he hadn't just watched the potential love of his life run out the door.

"I don't know. I'll let you know."

"All right. Try not to do anything too stupid in the meantime."

He laughed. "You know me."

She snorted. "Yeah, I do. That's why I said it."

"Bye, Iz. Thanks."

"Yeah, anytime. And Chris…think about what I said."

She hung up before he could say anything else.

She didn't have to worry. He was pretty sure every moment of the last several weeks was going to play out a million times in his head.

He flagged down a taxi and had it take him back to the house. It held no appeal for him now without Charley. Nothing did.

He sat down on the bed and repeated to himself all the reasons he should stay away from her. But he couldn't stop thinking about all the rest. The flash of her smile when she caught sight of him. The little wrinkle of concern she'd get when he was about to do something stupid. The sheer utter beauty of her when she lay in his arms.

Her lie could cause him a world of troubles. Then again, had she gone through with her analysis, he might have had to step down from his position anyway. And the thought of that… The thought of that was like a weight being lifted from his shoulders.

Suddenly, nothing else seemed to matter much except Charley. His business, hers, their differences, none of it mattered.

Only she did. He was going to have to figure out a way to convince her of that, which might be hard since he wasn't totally convinced of it himself.

But he had to try.

Chapter Seventeen

Charley turned side to side, checking herself out in Izzy's mirror while Cass sat on the bed watching.

They'd dressed her for the upcoming board meeting, and with the smart power suit hugging her curves, she thought she might almost be able to make it through with some semblance of dignity.

When she'd gotten a call from Chris's assistant asking her to come present her finalized assessment report to the board, she'd thought she'd heard wrong. Surely, they should be calling to fire her. Hell, she wouldn't have been surprised if they'd pressed charges. Instead, they seemed to be giving her a shot to salvage her career.

"This is crazy, right?" she turned around to ask the girls.

Izzy shrugged. "Maybe they pulled their heads out of their asses and realized you were the best there was so who you worked for didn't make any difference."

Charley rolled her eyes. "Right, I'm sure that's exactly what happened."

Cass laughed. "All that matters is that you look totally

fabulous."

Charley turned back to the mirror. She hoped so, because it would suck even harder if she looked bad while she got her ass handed to her.

"Come on, ladies!" Izzy said, standing and waving her hand toward the door. "We've got a meeting to crash."

Cass laughed and shook her head as Izzy sashayed her way out of the room. Then she turned back to Charley, who still hadn't moved.

"What's up?"

Charley bit her lip, feeling a little awkward talking about Chris to Cass. She was his ex after all, though she didn't seem remotely bothered by the fact that he and Charley had some weird thing going on.

"Do you think he'll be there?" she finally asked.

Cass gave her a knowing and sympathetic smile. "I'd imagine so."

Charley took a deep breath and nodded then pressed a hand to her somersaulting stomach. Cass came over and gave Charley's shoulders a light squeeze.

"Look, whatever else Chris is, he's a good guy. Even if he was mad enough to chew knives, he'd still be polite and respectful at the very least."

Charley nodded again. She knew that theoretically, but it felt better to hear someone else say it.

"Besides," Cass said, dropping her hands and reaching over to grab her sweater from the bed. "I don't think he's all that mad anymore. If he ever was. I don't think you have to worry about anything. Just go in there and give your report."

Charley opened her mouth to ask Cass how she knew that Chris wasn't angry, but Izzy called out to them from the front room that the car was there.

"Ready?" Cass asked.

"As I'll ever be, I guess," Charley said, taking another

deep breath.

She followed the other women to the elevator outside their penthouse and then to the car, trying not to fidget on the way to Chris's building.

"Are you going to recommend him?" Izzy asked.

Charley played with the edges of her that held the completed file on one Christopher Alexander Lachlan. "I'm not sure yet."

Izzy raised an eyebrow at that, and Charley sighed.

"Going strictly by the numbers, no, I shouldn't recommend him."

"But," Cass said.

"But…there's more to him than numbers."

Izzy flashed a megawatt grin at her.

"But," Charley said again. "That doesn't mean the numbers are wrong. If he wasn't…who he is…then I wouldn't be recommending him today. There are certain aspects of his life that are a little too risky for the insurance company. And they are who I'm technically working for."

"But if you don't recommend him…" Izzy said, and Charley nodded.

"If I don't, he has to step down." She groaned and put her face in her hands. "But if I do recommend him just because I care about him, then I'm proving all those people who would accuse me of trading sex for good scores right. Or whatever else they might say. And let's face it, very little stays secret in this world anymore. Someone is going to find out at some point, and if I do less than my best and give in because I don't want to hurt him, then I'm screwing myself in the long run."

Cass leaned over and rubbed her shoulder. "You do what you feel is right, Charley. Chris wouldn't want you to do anything less."

"Even if it means he loses his company?"

"Even that," Cass said, her voice so certain Charley

almost believed her.

The car pulled up to the building, and Charley took another deep breath, trying to calm the nerves having a rave inside her stomach. Cass opened the door and climbed out then stood waiting for Charley and Izzy.

"All right, let's do this," Charley muttered to herself. She straightened her spine, stuck her chin out, and marched into Lachlan Enterprises with her head held high. She knew what she had to do. The courage to do it might be lacking, but she'd fake it until she felt it. What other choice did she have?

The elevator doors dinged, and she marched into the office with Cass and Izzy in tow then stopped short. All of Chris's friends were sitting in the reception area. And all looked up almost in unison and gave her wide grins.

"Okay, no offense, guys, but that's a little creepy," she said.

Izzy laughed and jerked her chin toward the glass-enclosed conference room. "Go get 'em."

Charley swallowed and smoothed her hand down the front of her suit. Chris sat at the head of the long table, his eyes on her as she made her way across the office and to the conference room. She didn't pause outside like she wished she could but pushed the door open and entered. The table full of mostly older white men glanced at her, like a giant single-celled organism with multiple eyes.

"Have a seat," Chris said, gesturing to the other end of the table.

She released a silent sigh of relief that she wouldn't have to sit right next to him while she delivered her report.

Charley pulled out her files and went through everything, meticulously listing every number, explaining every graph, and going over in minute detail every aspect of her report and final decision. Which was...

"While I believe that with certain lifestyle modifications,

Mr. Lachlan would be an excellent candidate for coverage, I cannot at this time give him my recommendation."

There was an instant surge of voices, all muttering and talking together. They were surprised. Hadn't expected her to not recommend him. To be honest, she was a little surprised herself. She'd wanted to give him her recommendation. Badly. But to do so would have gone against everything she hoped she was, and in the end, she couldn't do it.

She finally risked a glance at Chris. But instead of the anger or surprise she expected to see, he smiled at her. What was going on? He should be furious. She had effectively ended his career or, at the very least, put a large dent in it. But yet, there he sat, smiling like he couldn't be happier.

The boardroom around her erupted into chaos. The insurance guy who'd been sitting by her side shook her hand and then got pulled away by a few the board members, who were trying desperately to spin what she had said into something that would save Chris's job.

She didn't want to stick around to see the aftermath of what she'd done. A cowardly move, sure, but the guilt ate at her. The last thing in the world she had wanted to do was hurt him in any way, but she couldn't in good conscience recommend him. Had he been anyone else, she wouldn't have hesitated to deny him coverage weeks ago. She'd already compromised herself enough letting it go on as long as she did.

Though she hoped she'd given him a little bit of a loophole when she'd said that if he made some minor modifications then she would recommend him. She hadn't been lying. If he would take a few more precautions then, while still engaging in some overly risky behavior, she could at least say with some certainty his activities wouldn't cost the insurance company any money.

The voices got louder and louder, beating at her frayed

nerves. She gathered up her materials and headed for the door. She wanted nothing more than to get out of there. Well, that wasn't true. What she wanted more than anything was Chris. She wanted to throw herself in his arms. Beg him to take her back to that beautiful house in Spain. Or back to Fiji where they could make love on the beach. She'd even welcome the ass-sand if they could go back to their fantasy life and never leave it.

She glanced over her shoulder at Chris to see him rising from his chair, but that only made her move faster. She wouldn't be able to hold it together if he confronted her in front of everyone.

"Quiet!" he said.

She didn't stick around. She pushed open the doors and walked out into the reception area, trying to make a beeline for the elevator. But Izzy and Company saw her coming and blocked her path.

"What are you doing, Iz?" she asked. "I want to get out of here."

Izzy pulled her in for a quick hug. "I know, Chuck, but trust me on this. You're gonna want to stick around for a minute."

She followed Izzy's gaze toward the conference room where whatever Chris was saying was causing quite a stir. The board members seemed to be somehow more agitated but less anxious all at the same time.

"What's going on?" Charley asked again.

Izzy grinned. "You'll see."

Charley glanced around at Chris's friends and their wives, but all she got was a collection of knowing grins. She didn't have to wait long to find out what was going on, though, because a couple minutes later, Chris burst out of the conference room at a dead run. He stopped so short when he saw her standing there it was like a cartoon character trying to stop and running in midair.

That billion-dollar smile of his lit up her heart and broke it all over again. God, she had to get out of there.

"Thanks guys," he said. "I thought I was going to have to chase her down."

"Naw, we got you," Brooks said, slapping him on the shoulder.

"Yeah, no worries," Cole said.

Harrison grinned. "We wouldn't miss this for the world."

"What are they talking about?" Charley asked.

Chris closed the distance between them and reached out to brush a thumb across her cheek. She swallowed past the sudden lump in her throat and gazed up at him.

He took her hands in his. "I have a proposal for you," he said.

Charley's mouth dropped open, and her stomach went on a rampage.

"Chris," she said, her voice thick with emotion. Why was he doing this? Especially here and now? She couldn't...she didn't want to hurt him even more, but she just couldn't...

She tried to pull her hands from his grasp, but he held on tight. "Relax," he said with a laugh. "You look like you're about to pass out."

She gave him a shaky laugh. He wasn't far from wrong.

"It's a business proposal," he said. And despite the fact that the last thing in the world she wanted was a marriage proposal, hearing him say it was business did disappoint her a little.

And he seemed to know that because he looked at her with an amused grin. "I don't think you're as opposed to the other kind as you'd like me to think. That's something we can talk about later. Probably much later and with a much smaller audience." He winked at her, and the tension in her gut eased. At least a bit. She let out a breath and waited for him to continue.

"Right now, as I said, I have a business proposal for you. I've never met anyone quite like you. You're not only one of the most organized, dedicated, job-oriented people I know, you also seem to really enjoy it. Before meeting you, I never would've believed that assessing risk for a living could bring anyone joy. But you're not only the best at what you do, you have the rare privilege of loving your job."

"Chris, I'm really sorry I couldn't give you the result you hoped for. But I couldn't go against—"

"I know," he said, smiling at her again. "I'm glad you didn't. You were right not to recommend me."

"Okay," she said with a small frown.

"You have a lot to bring to the table, Charley. I could really use you on my team."

Her frown deepened. "Doing what?"

"As of two minutes ago, I'm no longer the president and CEO of Lachlan Enterprises."

"Oh, Chris…I'm so sorry. Truly."

But he shook his head, his smile growing larger. "I'm not sorry. In fact, I haven't felt this good in years."

She cocked an eyebrow at him, but the mountain of guilt pressing on her chest eased up a little.

He squeezed her hands. "I've stepped down from my position, though I'll keep enough shares to keep me fabulously wealthy. And I'll still be a consultant for the board. I'm not going to completely lose anything, but I will no longer have to sit in boring board meetings and deal with all the day-to-day operation stuff that I can't stand. What I *will* get to do is focus more on the stuff that made me create this business in the first place. Traveling, finding new properties, scoping out new locations."

His excitement was palpable, and Charley couldn't help but smile. "Chris, that sounds amazing."

"It will be if you come with me."

Her jaw dropped, and her heart leaped in her chest. But she still wasn't sure what he was offering. "You want me to come as...an assistant?"

"No. As the company's resident risk assessor."

"What?" she asked.

"I'm going to be scouting new locations for company-held properties, checking on old ones, making sure everything is as it should be. My company facilitates home renting for the general public, but I make a good deal of money with privately owned luxury properties that we rent also. It's been a long time since I was able to focus on finding new places. And I haven't been able to keep as close an eye on my properties as I would like, which, as you know, has caused some problems. I can finally be more hands on, out in the field where I really want to be. And I can't think of anybody more perfect to be at my side than you."

"Me?" she asked, not sure what to think. As a job offer, it was amazing. It would obviously include a lot of travel, which triggered her insecurities a little. Still, though, who wouldn't love to travel the world in search of five-star accommodations?

But...was that the only reason he wanted her? Because as wonderful as it sounded, she didn't think she could be just an employee to him.

He squeezed her hands in his. "As you said, nobody does your job better than you. You are the best risk assessor out there. Who better to help me choose new properties for the company than someone who can spot the tiniest risk from ten miles away?"

He had a point. She was flattered. More than flattered. It was an incredible offer. But...

He tugged on her hands, pulling her into his arms, and she glanced up at him in surprise. "Besides," he said, tipping her chin up to keep her gaze on his. "I've never been great at the long-distance relationship thing. I don't think I could tear myself from your side if I tried. So, you'll just have to come with me, because I can't live without you."

Charley sucked in a breath. Had he really just said what she thought he said?

He gave her a soft smile that melted every bone in her body. "The risk assessor job is yours if you want it. But if you don't, that's fine, too. I just want you with me. And I know how much you love your job, so this seemed like the perfect solution. I'll be happy with whatever your decision is regarding the job. As long as you say yes to being with me. We'll make it work, whatever your decision. If you want me, that is."

She laughed, happiness, fear, excitement, and sheer adrenaline rushing through her so strongly her head spun. She wanted to say yes, so badly, but she was so afraid of disappointing him.

He brushed his lips across her cheek. "What's going on in that head of yours?" he asked so only she could hear.

She looked up into those gorgeous blue eyes of his. "It all sounds amazing. Too good to be true. But…I don't know if I can give you everything you might want."

His forehead creased slightly. "All I want is you."

"Yes but…we've never really discussed anything about a long-term relationship. Marriage, children, all that stuff. I'm happy with the way my life is. For the most part," she said, giving him a shy smile. "I've never been one of those girls who dreamed about what my wedding dress would look like or who had all my kids' names picked out. I'm not sure if I'll ever want any of that. I love my job. I want to focus on building my career. The other stuff…" She shrugged, hoping he'd understand.

His face smoothed out, all concern melting away. "We have time to work out all the details. I meant what I said,

Charley. All I want is you. If you don't ever want to get married, I'm cool with that. As long as we're together, that's all that matters. Kids…if my biological clock ever gets ticking, I'll go play with some of their kids," he said, jerking his thumb over at his friends, who were watching them like they were the best show ever. All they were missing was the popcorn. "Trust me, that'll kill the urge pretty quickly."

She laughed and leaned her forehead into his chest. He cradled her head in his hands and kissed the top of her head.

"If you decide you want kids later, awesome. It's not something I ever planned on, but let's face it, we'd make adorable babies."

She had to smile at that. He wasn't wrong.

"And if you never want kids, that's fine with me, too."

She glanced up at him again. "Are you sure?"

"I want *you*, Charley. That's it."

She took a deep breath and slowly let it out.

She loved him. So much it hurt. They didn't know each other well yet, but this was the first time she'd ever started a relationship without feeling the crushing pressure of expectations weighing against the risky odds that everything would go wrong. He wanted her. And she wanted him.

Simple. Easy. And perfect.

"I want you, too," she said, smiling up at him with all the love in her heart.

Epilogue

"This isn't really how I pictured us ending up," Brooks said, nodding at the scene before them.

Chris took a pull from his beer and laughed, shaking his head. "What? Are you telling me that the settled-down family life isn't for you?"

Brooks looked out in front of them where Kiersten, Leah, and Nikki were building sandcastles with a couple of the youngest kids while several older children ran around, splashing in the waves and throwing sand at each other under the watchful eyes of their mothers.

"Naw, I didn't mean that. It's just not how I thought it would be, that's all." He paused to take a long drink and then smiled. "It's better."

Chris raised an eyebrow, and Cole chuckled.

"Never thought I'd see the day," Harrison said. "Mr. Can't-Keep-It-In-His-Pants, blissfully happy as an old married man covered in kids."

"Damn straight," Brooks said, drawing another laugh from the group.

"And what about you?" Harrison asked, nodding at Chris. "Are you and Charley planning on kids anytime soon?"

Chris didn't bother to contain his groan. They'd actually made it a good two hours before the topic came up this time. He looked out to the ocean where his Charley was currently doing doughnuts on a jet ski with Izzy. Something he never would've imagined her doing a few years ago. Though Charley was still Charley. She'd heavily researched every make and model of jet ski available before they'd purchased them, made some sort of risk assessment spreadsheet, planned for every possible emergency, was wearing a life vest, and probably had six other emergency aids ready to go just in case.

But she *was* out there, having a blast. She'd simply figured out how to mix his love of adrenaline-spiked fun with her need to maintain safety. God, that woman was perfection.

Harrison cleared his throat, and Chris reluctantly tore his eyes away from the love of his life to glance at his boys, who were impatiently waiting for an answer. He narrowed his eyes behind his sunglasses and finally said, "Charley and I never plan on anything."

Cole snorted. "We've met Charley. That woman plans *everything*. She has plans for her plans. Literally."

Chris laughed. "For most things. When it comes to us and our future, though, we're happy going with the flow."

"Have you guys even discussed it?" Harrison asked.

Chris sighed. "Why are the men sitting around discussing kids and family planning? Shouldn't we be telling dick jokes and scratching our balls or something?"

Brooks rolled his eyes. "It's 2019, man."

Chris laughed. "Yes, we've discussed it. And again, we're both good with the way things are now. If she ever decides she wants kids, sure, I'd be down for it. I've never had a burning desire to procreate, but I want Charley to be happy. If it happens accidentally, then we'd be fine with that, too. It could be cool having a little mini running around. But I don't think we'll ever purposely try for a kid. We're good with how things are."

His friends had varying expressions of disappointment and understanding on their faces, which amused Chris to no end. They were worse than his mother. "Besides," he added, "what do we need our own kids for? We've got half a dozen godsons and daughters and counting." He nodded back at the group on the beach, a warm flow of affection flooding his chest. He wasn't lying. His friends were turning into little baby factories, and he and Charley were both more than happy to love on their godkids for a few days and then turn them back over to their parents. They had the best of both worlds.

"And you guys are still not planning on a wedding?" Cole asked.

Chris shrugged. "I doubt it. She's turned me down every time I ask, but I'm good with that. Again, it's up to her. We try to keep too much planning out of it. Discussing the what-ifs drive Charley a little crazy. As long as we are both happy, there's no reason to push for anything else just to make everyone else happy. We love our life."

"Wait…how many times have you asked?" Brooks asked.

Chris grinned. "Three, so far."

"And it doesn't bother you that she keeps saying no?" Harrison asked.

"Not even a little. As long as she's the first thing I see when I wake up in the morning and the last thing I see when I go to bed, I'm a happy man. If she wants to formalize things at some point, I'd be fine with that. If not, I'm happy as long as she's by my side. I propose to her every year on our anniversary, just in case. It's sort of become a tradition. She's racking up quite the ring collection."

Brooks raised an eyebrow. "You buy a new ring every

year?"

"Well, yeah. I can't propose with an old ring."

Cole laughed. "Well, I guess that's one way to get jewelry from your man."

Chris snorted. "That woman has me wrapped around every one of her fingers. I'd give her the world if she'd let me. But she's notoriously reluctant to accept extravagant presents. I've had to get creative to get those gifts in there. Next year I might propose with this cute little Tuscan villa she's had her eye on."

The guys all laughed, and Chris drained his beer and then leaned farther back in his chair, linking his hands behind his head. "Sorry to disappoint you, guys, but Charley and I are pretty happy just the way things are."

"What?" Cole said. "Traveling the world, stopping in for an occasional board meeting, spending your lives doing whatever you want whenever you want… Wait. That actually does sound pretty good."

"Yeah, sure," Brooks said. "But see, we got this pool going on when you two will finally make it legal…"

Chris rolled his eyes and groaned. "I hope somebody bet on never because it looks like that's what's going be happening."

He laughed at the chorus of groans and curses. "Sorry. We're together and stupidly, blissfully happy. What else do we need? A piece of paper isn't going to suddenly make everything different. She's mine. I'm hers. We're good."

"Well, I'm happy for you," Cole said. "Though that's going to make collecting on these bets difficult."

Chris laughed, not feeling remotely sorry for his friends. "I guess you guys will just have to keep that pool going."

Acknowledgments

First of all, thank you so much to my readers! You guys make it possible for me to do what I love, and I love each and every one of you. My deepest thanks to the amazing team at Entangled. Thank you to my wonderful editor, Alethea Spiridon, who loved this series as much as I did and helped make it something I truly love. I don't know what I'd do without you! Thank you so much for all your tireless work and support.

To Liz Pelletier and Jessica Turner for all your feedback and support. And Jessica, special thanks for all your meet cute help! I absolutely love how it turned out. Profuse and emphatic thanks to Riki Cleveland—Thank you so much for everything you do to get my books out in the world! And Holly Bryant-Simpson, thank you for everything you've done for me over the years! I've enjoyed working with you and am going to miss you!

To my sweet husband and amazing kids. You are my everything. Always. I love you so much. To my sweet family— thank you for being my biggest cheerleaders. I can't tell you what it means to know I always have you in my corner. I love you all!

To Toni, for your unwavering support and friendship, without which my world would be a dark and dreary place. To Sarah Ballance, for always being there when I need to vent and helping me keep all aspects of my life on track. Just… keep your spiders and all other terrifying things over in your own state! I'll play with the puppies and kitties, though! And to Naima Simone, thank you for making me laugh, being a sounding board, and helping me get through those writing sprints! I'm not sure I'd have finished this book without you.

And to the Small Town Titans, for inspiring Charley's rock session. If you haven't heard their version of "The Grinch," you must!

About the Author

USA Today bestselling author Kira Archer resides in Pennsylvania with her husband, two kiddos, and far too many animals in the house. She tends to laugh at inappropriate moments and break all the rules she gives her kids (but only when they aren't looking), and would rather be reading a book than doing almost anything else. Most of her non-writing hours are spent hanging with her family and running her kids around because they are busy and she's the taxi driver. She loves her romances a little playful, a lot sexy, and always with a happily ever after. She also writes historical romances as Michelle McLean.

Discover more swoony romance titles from Entangled…

THE BEST FRIEND PROBLEM
a *Mile High Happiness* novel by Mariah Ankenman

All that's missing from Pru's life is a baby. Luckily, it's the twenty-first century—she can take matters into her own hands. Until Pru goes in for a fertility check-up to find…she's already pregnant. With her best friend's baby. As best friends, Pru and Finn have survived college, new jobs, and bad breakups, but can they survive crib shopping, birth classes, and late-night cravings? Especially when Finn has never considered himself even remotely Daddy material?

BETRAYING THE BILLIONAIRE
an *Abbott Sisters* novel by Victoria Davies

Julian Worth isn't a man with time to spare. Ruling his billion-dollar empire with an iron fist, work is the true love of his life. Which is why when it comes to marriage, a strategic alliance matters more than love. Julian is more than ready to sign on for a little superficial dating and a marriage of convenience if it allows him to take his company to the next level. What he wasn't ready for was the woman who shows up as his prospective bride. What he doesn't know, is she isn't who she pretends to be.

How To Lose a Fiancé
a novel by Stefanie London

Sophia has always been the "good daughter" who tried to keep her domineering father happy. She followed the rules and did everything that was asked of her. But this time, her father is asking too much. The family company is crumbling, and her father has arranged a marriage to a Greek billionaire who can save their business. If Cinderella can dress up to win a prince, surely Sophia can do the opposite and ditch hers...

Catching the Player
a *Hamilton Family* novel by Diane Alberts

Kassidy Thomas didn't quite bet on singing a horrible song in front of the handsomest bachelor in the NFL, Wyatt Hamilton. She also doesn't think he'd then consequently ask her out on a date. Married to the game, Wyatt Hamilton has no interest in relationships, love, or even second nights with the same woman. But from the second the girl-next-door beauty Kassidy knocks on his door to deliver a singing telegram, nothing goes as planned. He can't stop thinking about her, and keeps showing up on her doorstep for more. That is, until the unthinkable happens...And all bets are off.

Made in the USA
Coppell, TX
11 April 2020